Holy Smoke

Also By Alexandra Eden

To Oz and Back

HOLY SMOKE

a **Bones & the Duchess** Mystery

Alexandra Eden

ALLEN A. KNOLL, PUBLISHERS

SANTA BARBARA, CA

Allen A. Knoll, Publishers, 200 West Victoria Street,
Santa Barbara, CA 93101
(805) 564-3377
bookinfo@knollpublishers.com

First Edition, Second Impression
07 06 05   5   4   3   2

This is a work of fiction. The characters and events por-
trayed in this book are fictitious, any resemblance to real
people or events is coincidental.

Library of Congress Cataloging-in-Publication Data

Eden, Alexandra.
    Holy smoke : a Bones & the duchess mystery / Alexandra Eden-- 1st ed.
        p. cm.
    Summary: Bones Fatzinger, a former police officer, teams up again with Verity
Buscador, a clever twelve-year-old with Asperger's syndrome, to investigate a mysterious
church fire.
    ISBN 1-888310-46-4 (alk. paper)
    [1. Asperger's syndrome--Fiction. 2. Arson--Fiction. 3. Mystery and detective stories.] I.
Title.

PZ7.E22Ho 2004
[Fic]--dc22

                                                          2003066106

Printed by Sheridan Books in Chelsea, MI
text typeface is Goudy 13 point
Smyth sewn case bind with Skivertex Series 1 cloth

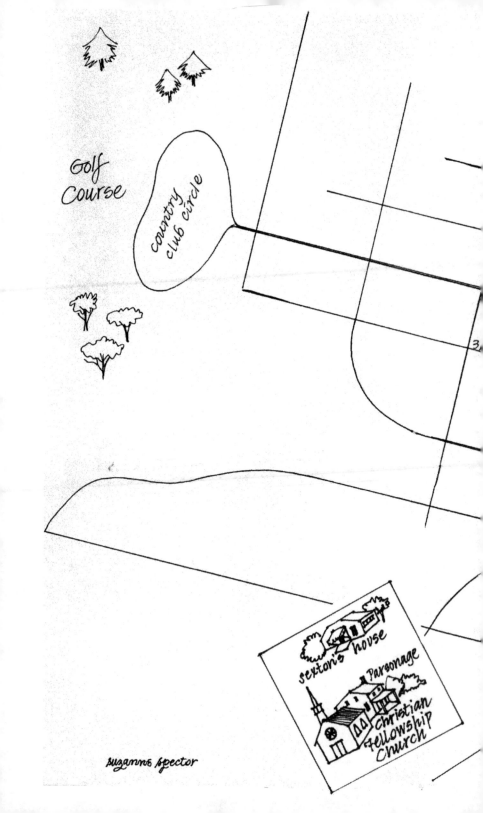

Golf
Course

country
club circle

3,

sexton's house

Parsonage

christian
fellowship
Church

suzanne spector

The Borough of Ephesus

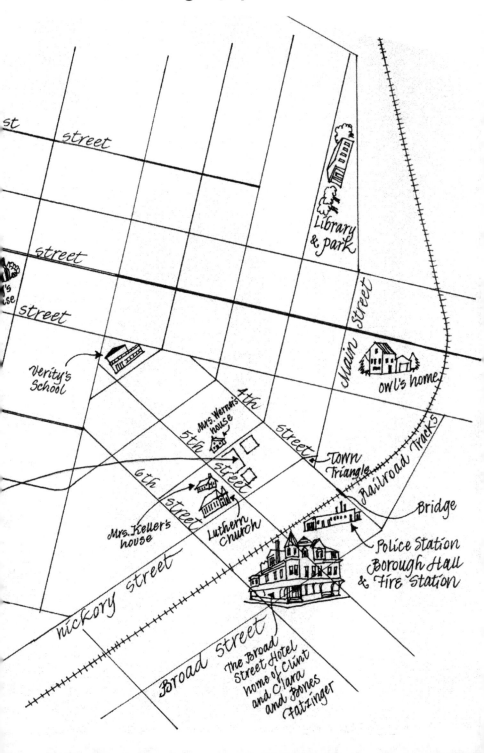

One

"Holy smoke, the church is on fire!" It was the duchess talking.

We were standing across the street from the blaze on Fifth Street, a couple of blocks from the Broad Street Hotel, where I make my home and where the duchess's grandmother and grandfather run the show. It was warm for a September evening. The fire made it hot.

The duchess sometimes overstates the obvious, as in this case, where the Christian Fellowship Church was being consumed by hungry flames leaping up to the heavens as though begging for attention.

The fire department was out in force. Since Ephesus was a small Pennsylvania town, the fire department was manned by volunteers. They all had pagers and cell phones—and could show up or not. Since fires around here were rare, most of the volunteers showed up. That means somewhere around 30 guys running around in rubber coats and galoshes or big boots.

I knew most of the firemen because I used to be a policeman in town, and the police station was connected to the fire station.

The firemen took turns manning the fire station—a big garage-like room with a big red fire truck, a smaller van for getting around in if they didn't need a big truck, and an ambulance operated by paramedics. All this equipment was bought with donations from the townspeople. There were two paramedics on duty, one who had training and one who helped. With the two firemen, there were four people hanging out at the fire station most of the time. It was enough to play hearts or pinochle. If there were fewer they played gin rummy. There was hardly a time in the day when the volunteer firemen and the paramedics weren't playing cards. It was like belonging to an exclusive club in Ephesus.

I asked one of my old buddies Emory Wentz what happened.

"Not sure yet," he said. "Looks like someone started it in the basement."

"That easy to do?" I asked. "Start a fire in the basement of a brick building and get out before you are trapped?"

"It's a risk," he said. "Stairwell acts like a chimney. Whenever someone plays with fire they are in danger."

It was getting so hot across the street that we all moved down until the heat became bearable. There were a collection of neighbors on the sidewalk with the Reverend and Mrs. Ringer. He looked angry—the frown on his face pushed his black, bushy eyebrows closer together. His wife Grace was sobbing. Their home joined the church, and everyone wondered if that would catch on fire too. The firemen were trying hard to keep the house from burning.

There was a kid with the reverend and Mrs. Ringer who looked a couple years younger than Verity. That's who I called the duchess. Verity Buscador. The kid was jumping all over the place as though this were just the best entertainment.

He was a wiley little kid, not as tall as the duchess—one of those children who can't sit still, who is always driving adults nuts. If we lived in a bigger town they would probably put him on some pill to calm him down.

Danny Ringer came bouncing over to Verity.

"Hi, Verity," he said. "What's up?"

"Holy smoke," she said, "the church is on fire!"

Maybe you think, 'holy smoke, the church is on fire!' is a juvenile joke, but the duchess *is* as juvenile as they come—twelve years old. She has Asperger's Syndrome, this strange disease that messes up her nerves. She's bright as a whip but is a little different from the run-of-the-mill kid her age. She has a hard time making friends, so I try to be her friend. It isn't always easy. She got such a blast out of helping me on my first case, *To Oz and Back*, I'm afraid she's going to continue to hang around, messing with my cases. I was just going to have to be nice but firm and bring the duchess back to earth after she broke the codes in that case and all. Otherwise she'd be a permanent fixture in my opera.

The duchess was staring straight ahead like she always did, and she didn't talk much. But when she did it was in this straight, flat tone—like a clarinet playing only one note.

The duchess pretty much ignored Danny and

when he scurried away, she said to the air—straight ahead—"Danny did it."

"What?" I exclaimed. "Did what? Started this fire? No way. The minister's son? What is he—nine or ten years old?"

"He's as old as I am."

"Well, so what? Would you go around burning your parents' house?"

"This isn't their house. It's a church."

"All well and good," I said, "but you will notice that their house is in danger. Maybe Danny likes to sleep in the street?"

She said nothing, which was what she usually did when I tied her in knots with my logic.

I looked over at the Ringer family, and the parson caught my eye, and it seemed to give him an idea. He came over to where I was standing with the duchess.

"Fatzinger, is it?" he said, putting out a grim hand for me to shake. I did it.

"Reverend," I said, "I'm so sorry about this fire."

"You're staying at the Broad Street—with Clint and Clara, aren't you?"

"I live up there these days," I admitted. It was a nice enough hotel, but it wasn't going to win me any points on the social scale.

"The girl here—Verity—and you, of course, did some good work on that case with the two missing girls."

I wanted to thank him, but it stuck in my throat—him mentioning the duchess first like that.

"Think you could help out with this?"

"Well, I..."

"We can," the duchess chimed in, and I was *so* embarrassed. All I could think of was to wink at the parson.

"Come to see me in the morning," he said, then added, "if you're interested." He looked at the flames, which the firemen had gotten under some control. "Say, nine or ten o'clock?"

"Where?" I asked, looking across the street.

"Good question. We'll probably be spending the night with the sexton—firemen suggested we let the fire cool down. I expect we'll be back in the house in the morning. Let's say ten to be safe."

"You think the firemen have it under control?"

He tightened his jaw, looking grimly at the dying fire—"I think the house is safe. Whoever did this wanted only the church."

Two

The sun was out the next morning, but there was still smoke in the sky.

The firemen had put out the fire in the church before it spread to the Ringer's house, which they called the parsonage.

I was up early for breakfast, so I had it in the dining room of the Broad Street Hotel with its owners and operators Clint and Clara Rudy. I was getting used to the country scenes painted on the walls of the room. The hotel faced south so when the sun was out the room was cheery—it was just peeking over the south mountain when we sat down to one of Clara's breakfast feasts. Bacon, eggs, fried potatoes, ham, toast, jam, cereal if you want it.

"That was some fire last night," I said.

I didn't get an argument, but I didn't get any opinions either. "So," I asked, "what do you make of it?"

"A sadness," Clara said. Clint didn't argue. "Clint?"

"I don't like it one bit. This is not the kind of town where you expect people to go around burning churches. Bad for our reputation—bad for business."

"Who do you suppose would do something like that?"

"Beats me. I hope it was someone from out of town, but who knows?"

Clara said, "I expect it's someone doesn't like their brand of religion."

"Could it be someone doesn't like the Reverend Ringer?"

"Could be anything," Clara said.

"I don't see Sterling Ringer making any enemies hereabouts," Clint said. "He's a good fellow—comes to Rotary here every week. Got a smile on him won't quit. He's got to sell his brand of religion. The Lutherans and Congregationalists have this town pretty well sewed up. Their ministers can coast—the others have a struggle."

"So there wouldn't be any need for one of those church members to want to put the Reverend Ringer out of business?"

"Not that I can see," Clint said.

Clara was shaking her head. "People who hurt others—burn down churches and such in the name of strange religion—don't have their heads screwed on straight."

I almost told them the theory proposed by Verity, their granddaughter, but I knew they loved her, and I didn't want to make fun of her.

Getting up from the table after any of Clara's feasts was always a challenge.

If it hadn't been for the railroad tracks being fenced off, I could have walked down the street from the Broad Street—one straight shot of three blocks—

but I had to go a block over to cross the bridge at my old stomping grounds, the police station, and borough hall. Ephesus, our town, was called a borough because it was so small—somewhere around 6,000 folks.

It was a sad sight indeed, coming upon the church burned out to nothing but brick walls, and those were not whole. You wouldn't think fire could burn bricks, but it burned all the support—even melted metal it was so hot—and things fell against the wall, and the firemen knocked down parts of it in an effort to save some of the church—but they never did.

The parson's house was covered with black soot from the fire. What used to be red bricks was now just dirty black.

Verity was safely in school, so I was able to talk to Parson Ringer alone.

He opened the front door, and what I might call a smile of relief came to his face.

"Ah, Fatzinger," he said almost as though he'd forgotten his invitation from the night before. "Come in."

The small room was dark—the windows were covered with soot—ashes had blown inside and were being cleaned up by Mrs. Ringer, the minister's wife.

"Bad business," he said, shaking his head. "This is *bad* business."

"Yes it is," I said, "I'm so sorry it happened."

"Thank you."

"Any ideas on how it started?"

"Oh, it was arson," he said. "Someone started it—the firemen are sure of that."

"Any idea who?"

He licked his lips, giving the smile a short rest. His forehead creased in thought as though it were the first time he'd considered who it might have been.

Grace Ringer was vacuuming the floor under our feet. "Sorry," she said, "sorry about this. I wanted to get this before you came—but so many people have called to express their condolences…"

"Maybe Mr. Fatzinger wouldn't mind if you waited until he left."

"That's okay," I said, "either way."

"I just don't feel right having my home on display looking like this."

"And the vacuum does make a lot of noise," the Reverend said, "We're trying to talk."

"It'll only take a minute."

Grace Ringer was a world-class vacuum cleaner—so thorough I thought the vacuum would suck up the carpet. Then she turned to the furniture and the ashes flew all over the place.

The reverend was definitely not smiling. "I'm sorry about this," he said. "Ordinarily we'd meet in the church study." He looked at his wife, vacuuming away. "Perhaps we should go outside."

With that Grace turned off the machine as though on cue. I had a thought that maybe she wanted to hear what we said, and if we were outside she wouldn't be able to.

No sooner had she turned off the vacuum and said, "There, the noise is over," than she pulled a cloth from I don't know where and began dusting the furniture.

"Grace, please—may we have a bit of privacy?"

"Oh, I won't be in the way," she said. "I won't listen a bit."

Reverend Ringer looked over at me with a grim smile, as if to say, what are you going to do?

"Well, it's certainly been hot hereabouts," the reverend said, "I'll say that."

"Yes."

"Of course September is not always a cool month, I'll say that."

"No."

"You from around these parts, Mr. Fatzinger?"

"Oh, call me Bones—everyone else does."

"Well, it's shorter, I'll say that."

"Yes."

"Bones."

"Yes. I am from these parts—born over in New Tripoli," I said. I pronounced it like the locals—Trip-*pole*-ee, instead of the original over in Europe or Africa somewhere—Trip-o-*lee*.

"That so?"

"Yes."

"New Tripoli—well I'll be."

"Yes."

"Nice town?"

"Oh yes. How about yourself?"

"We hale from the Tamaqua area. In this calling we get moved so much you never really know where you'll wind up next. It has its advantages, I'll say that."

"What are they?"

"Oh, you don't go stale in a place—always a

10

new challenge—new people to meet and bring to the faith."

"Make any enemies along the way?"

Sterling Ringer frowned, and his wife twitched. I could see by the reverend's face that he didn't want to talk about it in front of his wife, so we sat there making small talk until there was not one surface in the tiny room that didn't sparkle.

"Well, Mr. Fatzinger, that will have to do for now," Grace said, "It was nice to meet you."

The reverend kept his eyes on her until she left the room.

"Oh, Honey," he sang out.

"Yes?" She reappeared at the door with a look of expectation on her face—as though her husband had decided to include her in the conversation after all.

"Would you close the door, please?"

Her sunny face fell like a sudden sundown, but she shut the door.

Three

"I'm sorry to have to make you wait like that M...ah, Bones. Grace is a dear, sweet soul, but she does like to talk."

And listen, I thought.

"And I'd like our discussion to be confidential, if that's all right with you?"

I nodded. "I always keep my dealings with clients confidential."

"Good."

Reverend Sterling Ringer wore a bow tie. Not many men in Ephesus wore bow ties. It was something that set him apart. He was, along with his wife Grace, very heavy—but in Ephesus that didn't set you apart. Everyone in Ephesus, it seemed, was heavy—yours truly included.

Even the Ringers' wiry kid Danny was heavy for his age.

"Well, I don't have to tell you what a sorry thing this fire is for this church and its mission in Ephesus and the world over, I'll say that."

I noticed for the first time when the reverend talked his bow tie bounced with the movement of his Adam's apple—that part of his body that stuck out from his flabby neck. As a result of this entertainment, while he talked, my eyes were not on his eyes as they should have been, but on his neck and dancing bow tie. I noticed the more excited Reverend Ringer got, the faster and jerkier the bow tie danced.

"It is bad enough," he continued, "to be the victim of such an act of hate...an act of hate," he repeated, "I'll say that. But it may be worse not to know who did it and why. The motive is very important to me, I'll say that. Is it an act directed against our beliefs, or is it an act directed against me? I would just like to sit down with this firebug and find out what was on his mind."

"Or her," I said.

"Her? Oh, I don't think a woman...no. Women are more gentle souls, I'll say that. You don't find women burning churches. But I suppose anything is possible. No, I want to sit face to face with this...person. I want to look into this person's heart. I want to understand how anyone could sink so low as to do this to a fellow human being. Why? I'll ask why again and again until I get an answer."

The reverend looked at me as though he were slightly surprised to see me. "Oh yes," he said, his bow tie bobbing, "that's where you come in. I want you to find this man...woman...or persons and bring him— her—them—to me. It could be more than one person, I'll say that." He looked me in the eye. The bow tie was at rest, so I looked in his eye. "Can you do it? For me? For my church?"

"I can try," I said. "But first, don't you want to wait to see what the police find out?"

"The police? Oh, I don't expect too much from

the police. It's a small town—not many resources. I don't think I'll get much from the police. Even if I do, I may not want the embarrassment of what they find to be made public."

"You can tell them that."

He spread his hands apart. "But how can I do that? They'll want to prosecute, this firebug will have a soap box for his opinions, his hate will be made public, and maybe give others the same idea—burn churches, any church that is different from yours."

"How can I stop that?"

"You can *bring* him to me. I'm a Christian. I turn the other cheek. I don't care about prosecuting. An eye for an eye...and the whole world goes blind. The police are overworked. You should understand how I feel. You were asked to leave the Ephesus Police Department for the same human feelings I have—some poor woman shoplifted from the super market because she didn't have enough for her family to eat. Your boss wanted you to arrest her, but you paid her bill instead. Those of us beholden to a higher power sided with you. What earthly good would it do to put that poor woman in jail? Who would feed her children then?"

I nodded. I must say it was nice to hear someone take my side in the matter.

"You don't have a family, do you, Bones?"

"No, but I do have to live—were you thinking of...paying anything for this detective work?"

"Oh, I don't have any illusions anyone in your line would do this for the glory of God, or the good of mankind. We'll expect to pay, I'll say that. How much will be a matter of negotiation—an agreement between us."

Hm, I thought. That was some build up to get me to keep my price down—good of mankind and all that. If I asked more than he thought I should, I'd be working against the good of society. I needed the work, there was no arguing with that. Trouble was, he knew I needed it.

"How much do you think a job like this would be worth...in the private sector?"

Private sector? I thought. He was talking about working for someone—not a church. If I told him a number—amount of money—for that, he'd ask for the religious discount. Then I should tell him in my religion we didn't give discounts. But I didn't think he'd find that funny.

"How much would you pay?"

"How much do you want?"

"You tell me."

"Oh, no. If I hire a plumber he tells *me* what he charges. I don't tell him what I'll pay."

"Okay," I said. "How about this? You and I agree I was unfairly let go from the police department. Why not just pay me what a policeman earns in the same time. You are getting your own private detective wholesale—what it costs the bureau."

He smiled—and when Reverend Ringer smiled, his big round basketball face lit up like a neon sign over the drug store. "Fair," he said, "I'll say that. It's a deal then?"

"I suppose so."

"Oh—one other thing."

"What's that?"

"That little girl—the one that helped in your case with the two missing girls. What was her name?"

"Verity," I said, afraid of what was coming, "Verity Buscador."

"Yes, Verity," he said expressing pleasure at the thought. "I hear she was quite a help in that case—lot of folks say she was the one solved it."

I must have turned the color of a red beet. I opened my mouth to protest that idea, then closed it again. I thought I was doing Verity a favor being a pal to her. She didn't really have any friends of her own—the Asperger's thing she had made it difficult for her to make friends. So here was the reverend wanting me to let the duchess tag along. I wondered how long it would be until she was the one they hired and I was asked to tag along—or even worse—they hired *her* without me.

I guess since she was only 12, that wouldn't come too soon.

So we agreed on the price and on getting Verity's "help." Then I asked him for his theories and any suspects he had in mind.

"My suspicion is it is a faceless man with a lot of hate in his heart—possibly someone we don't know. He could be a member of another more established church wanting to keep other ideas out of town. It could be someone we know who is holding some kind of grudge—though I can't say I can recall an incident so bad that would make this happen. It could be someone who just had too much to drink at the Mercantile Club, two blocks down the street—someone who feels unappreciated by his wife, someone who feels he is without power in life and this is his twisted way of thinking he's powerful. Beyond that I just don't know. That's where you come in."

I'd almost been hypnotized by his dancing bow tie when he snapped me out of it with this charming thought, "Oh, and don't forget to get Verity to help. She might solve this one too—I'll say that."

Four

I left the Reverend Ringer without telling him that his beloved Verity thought Reverend Ringer's son Danny burned down his church. I wanted to do it, but I just couldn't. I realized he would not have thought Verity was off base, he would blame it on me for taking seriously an offhand remark, made without any evidence.

On my way back to the Broad Street Hotel, I stopped off at the police and fire station to check in with my old buddy Grumbera. We used to be policemen together, before I was asked to leave for paying for that poor woman's groceries instead of arresting her. I suppose I could have done both, I just didn't see any sense in making it any harder for her than she already had it.

Grumbera was at his desk looking like a royal potato. Grumbera is the Pennsylvania Dutch word for potato, and he loved to eat potatoes in any shape they came—raw, baked, mashed, boiled, scalloped, au gratin, parslied and especially fried in a ton of butter. We pronounced it *Grum*-bear-uh.

"How's it goin', Grumbera?" I said, greeting him with a hearty friendship.

"Goin' good, Bones."

He didn't bother to ask me how I was. Not a good sign.

"That was some fire last night at the church, wasn't it?"

"Yes it was."

"Got any suspects?"

"Not really."

"Ideas?"

"Yeah, I got ideas," Grumbera said, then clammed up.

"What kind of ideas?"

Grumbera looked at me as though he thought I was going to pick his pocket or something. Finally, after staring me down like he shouldn't have stared down an old comrade in arms in Ephesus law enforcement, he said, "I got an idea you got hired on the case and are here to pick my brain so you don't have to wear out yours."

I have to say that surprised me. Grumbera used to be my buddy. Someone must have put a bug in his ear, because he wouldn't treat me like that otherwise. It had to have been the chief.

"Not very friendly, Grumbera," I said, trying to show him with the sad expression on my face how disappointed I was.

"Yeah, well, the chief, you know, thinks you just cause trouble."

"You mean he doesn't want any competition solving cases—even if it makes it easier and faster?"

"Chief thinks you're just a private citizen, which you are, and maybe it's time you face that, Bones."

"Yeah," I said, "maybe I should."

"Be a good idea."

"Maybe I should just set in the rocker and rock back and forth, watching the sun cross the south mountain and suck my thumb."

Grumbera seemed surprised. "I don't know about that thumb part."

"What would you have me do instead?"

"Well, you could get a job for starters."

"Yeah, got any idea where?"

"Sure. You could work security over by the truck factory, the department store, the mall."

"Rent-a-cop? I suppose I could sell hot dogs and popcorn at football games, or maybe bag groceries down by the market."

"Sorry, Bones," Grumbera said. "I got my orders."

"All right, old buddy, if that's the way it has to be, that's the way it has to be. You tell me nothing, I find something out, I don't share it." I turned to go, "See you around, Grumbera."

"Yeah," he said.

I went out the door into the street without looking back. I turned into the big open garage door where the big red fire truck stood ready for the next big fire.

Frank Nonnemacher was on duty alone, there being a truckload of firemen tuckered out from fighting the big one last night at the church. He seemed happy to have someone to talk to.

"Getting over the fire?"

"Yeah," he said, "I was working the night shift

last night, so I missed it. That's how come I can come in this morning."

"Oh, so you don't know anything?"

"Only what I hear, and I hear it was a doozie."

"Yeah, I was across the street watching."

"Not pretty," he said.

"No," I said. "Well, you know, fire is a pretty dramatic color. Like the sun, which is just a huge fireball. I hear the guys who start these things for kicks are usually in the crowd watching."

"Or watching from somewhere, if they're not so foolhardy's to be right at the scene. My guess is a small town like this where he'd be recognized right off, why if he was watching, it was from somewhere he couldn't be watched in return."

"Yeah," I agreed. "So what are the theories going around?"

"Nothing concrete. The reverend is a very friendly-seeming guy, but I hear tell he may have some enemies. I wouldn't know personally, because I don't know much about him—seems there's always that big smile on his face, and that's about all I know. I'm a Lutheran myself."

"Why would a guy trying so hard to please people make enemies?"

"You never know what goes on in the mind of man. Could be someone in his church out of joint because of something he said in a sermon or something. There's just no telling."

"Talk to Grumbera about it?"

"Yeah, we shot the breeze this morning when I came on."

"They have any ideas?"

Frank grinned at me. "I guess if he did he didn't share them with you, seeing's I just saw you come out of there."

"Heck, Frank, you know my history with the department. The chief gets all touchy."

"I know, Bones," he said. "I think you got a raw deal. But Grumbera's on the spot—he doesn't want to go the way you did, he's got to toe the line, do what his boss says."

"Yeah, maybe I'll get him off guard some day at Clint's ice cream parlor. Grumbera likes ice cream."

"Grumbera likes *everything* from the look of him," Frank said. "Well, coming to think of it, he did mention the chief was talking to the bartender at the Mercantile Club. Rumor Tiny Bergstresser was acting funny last night."

"Thanks, Frank. It'll give me a start."

Five

When I got back to the Broad Street Hotel, Clint was in the Soda Fountain tidying up. It had been a bar-room, but someone had left a party there and had a car accident and died. The next day Clint took out all the alcohol and equipment and changed it to an ice cream soda fountain.

He put three signs on the wall that said:

Drinking is not cool.
Smoking is suicide and there are faster ways.
Drugs are for dumbells.

I went from the front parlor to the soda fountain on the right. Up at the counter I said, "How's it goin', Clint?"

"Can't complain," he said, running a rag over the counter.

He stopped his arm motion with the rag. "So, the reverend hired you?"

I couldn't tell if he was happy about that, so I nodded gently.

He nodded too and resumed polishing the counter. "You know how much Verity, my little grand-daughter, enjoyed helping you on your first case—and here you are with another one. That's good work."

"Thanks."

"I sure do love that little kid," Clint said. "Things can't be easy for her—she doesn't have a lot of friends, has trouble riding a bike, but she's smart as a whip. You know, she helped you out a lot."

"Yeah, well..." I knew what was coming.

"You know, Bones, I look the other way when your room and board payments are late. Clara rides me about it, so do yourself a favor—and me too of course—and let Verity help out again."

"Yeah, well, I'd love her too, but she's only twelve years old, and...darn it all Clint, she's *different*. And different is difficult. It's not that I don't get a kick out of hanging out with her, but it does bug me a little when I hear folks giving her a lot of the credit for solving the last case."

"Wasn't there something about codes?" Clint asked.

"There was."

"Didn't Verity—and that pal of hers with the glasses—didn't they crack the code?"

"Well, we did it together. I'm not looking to take any credit from her, but I'm an ex-cop. I know my way around—to suggest that I owe it all to a twelve year old takes credit from me."

"But, Bones, what do you care? You know what's done and who does it."

"People making me small. Everything I do I owe to a twelve year old!"

"No, no, come on, Bones, be a big guy. You mean you don't want the little input she can give you?

Want to go it alone?"

"Ach, Clint, listen, that parson—the Reverend Ringer—likes Verity too. He asked me to take her on. And since he's paying, how could I say no?"

"Good! Well, it's settled then," Clint said. "How about a root beer float?"

"Well...I...don't..."

"It's on the house."

"Yeah, sounds like a good idea."

Clint served up a root beer float for each of us. We sat at one of his cute ice cream parlor tables next to the window.

"Advertising," Clint said.

"What?"

He waved at the window. "We're advertising the place. People see you in the window."

"But not that many people walk by the Broad Street," I said. "Ever regret giving up the barroom?"

"Never!" he said. "Oh, I made a lot more money, I can't deny that, but this is so much better." He shook his head. "I used to have a place full of drunks. What a drag! Why do people want to put things in their bodies that make them stupid? It seems to me they are stupid enough."

"I'll drink to that," I said raising my root beer float. After I took a swallow and wiped the foam off my lips with the paper napkin that had *Broad Street Ice Cream Parlor* printed on it, I asked Clint, "Any new thoughts about the fire?"

"I been thinking all right—could be someone drunk out of his mind on booze. Could be someone couldn't stand Reverend Ringer or his brand of religion."

"The fireman says the fire started in the basement of the church. How many people you figure can get into that basement?"

"Probably anybody. I don't think Sterling Ringer ever locked that door to the basement."

"What about Bergstresser? Think he could have done it?"

"The town drunk? I don't think he's ever been violent, and I can't imagine him having a grudge against the reverend."

"Know anyone who does?"

"Well, there are these religious types that think their way is the only way," Clint said. "There's Josh Hinkle, he's pretty narrow, and I hear he's a bit of a hothead. Manny Lichtenwalner wants everyone to be a Lutheran just like him. I also hear tell of Reverend Fowler over at the Baptist church being somewhat narrow-minded about other faiths."

"Sterling Ringer says everything is hunky-dory. But he wants to make sure I go right to him and to him only with anything I find."

"He's going to hog-tie you before you begin. I can't believe he thinks everything is a-okay. I think you have to get him to loosen up before you begin. Save you a lot of time. Why, I wouldn't be surprised if he *knew* who did it."

"Says not."

"You need someone who can open the Reverend Ringer up—someone who knows him inside and out. You know," he said, surprised that he had such a good idea, "that boy of his is about Verity's age. Maybe she can find a lead there."

"Verity told me she thought he did it."

"Who, the boy?"

I nodded.

"Oh, I think that might be going too far. I hear he's a bit of a wild kid, but these days, wild kids aren't in short supply. But then who knows? These days nothing would surprise me."

I thanked Clint for the root beer float and went into the dining room for lunch—Clara's famous ham and string beans. Lot of people skim the fat off these dishes that are bound to have a lot of fat in them. Not Clara. "Takes all the taste out of it when you do that," she says.

After lunch I sat on the rocker on the front porch and watched the world go by. While I was trying to figure what my investigation was going to be I fell asleep in the chair. I awoke to the sound of footsteps on the steps to the porch. It was the duchess lugging her books and what have you. Her backpack was always so full I thought she must have her desk in there too.

The duchess's eyes were straight ahead as always, and she marched right by me into the hotel, saying, "I need an ice cream soda." She went in the front door and turned right into the soda fountain.

I followed.

Six

When I got into the ice cream parlor, Clint was lifting Verity's backpack off her shoulders, saying, "You don't want to sit on that." The duchess just never seemed to think of that.

Clint made the duchess a strawberry ice cream soda. He offered me one, but I didn't think I could just keep taking sodas from him, so I said, "Oh, no thanks."

The duchess concentrated on her soda while I took the chair facing her at the same table Clint and I had sat at next to the window.

"Advertising," the duchess said. Apparently Clint had said the same to her.

"Did you talk to Danny Ringer?" I asked while she was concentrating on the soda.

She didn't answer. I should have known better than to interfere with an activity she had her mind set on. I'd just have to sit it out until she was finished.

When she took the last slurp and inspected the bottom of the glass to make sure there was truly none left, I asked my question again, "Did you talk to Danny Ringer?"

"So you want my help?"

"Well, of course."

"We're going to be partners again?"

I looked over at Clint. He was smiling.

"Yes, yes, it's all settled."

"Danny wants to help too."

"Danny? Help?"

"Yes."

"But didn't you say you thought he started the fire himself?"

"Yes."

"So how does he fit? I mean, how can he help investigate himself?"

"He can help with other things. Then we can catch him."

"What can he help with?"

"Lots of things. Like he is in the church. He knows what happens. Danny says his father knows who did it, but he is just so goody-goody, he will never speak ill of anyone even if they burned down his church. That's why Reverend Ringer wants us to solve it, so he won't have to."

I don't think I believed that. Maybe he had suspicions, but he wasn't sure. Maybe if I went to him with theories he would correct me and eventually put me on the right path.

"Who does Danny's father think did it?"

"He won't tell me until we agree to let him help."

"Oh, more blackmail," I said.

"Sounds like a small price to pay," Clint said, washing some glasses. "You might get something out of him the police won't."

"The police? You know they turned a cold shoulder to me. I solved that missing girl case and threw it in their laps and gave them all the credit. I go to see Grumbera this time and he talks to me like a stranger. Says the chief is mad at me."

"Well, you don't think you showed him up, Bones?" Clint asked from behind the counter. "You and Verity brought him the kidnapper. *He* didn't do it, *you* did. That can't make him look too good."

"I used to *work* there, for goodness' sake. I'm family."

"*Was*," Clint said. "You did things differently. You and the chief were always at odds, so you can't be surprised he doesn't want you to show him up a second time."

"But Grumbera—Grumbera and I were *pals!*"

"Grumbera wants to get along. He knows to get along you have to go along—so he goes along with his boss."

Verity pushed the soda glass to the side. "Are you ready," she asked, "to get started on the case?"

"Well sure, I've started."

"What did you do?"

I might have said something sarcastic about *me* being the boss of *this* operation, but Clint was standing right there, and he wouldn't have appreciated it. Maybe I'd have to go along to get along. So I told her. "For starters, I got *hired*—*us* hired," I corrected myself. "Then I went to my old, should I say, *ex-pal*

Grumbera, and got nothing. I stopped by the fire station and found out from my friend Frank Nonnemacher that the fire was started in the basement, and the only suspect they can come up with is the town drunk."

"Did anyone in the neighborhood see anything?" the duchess asked.

"Well, I haven't gotten around to that," I said sheepishly. But why should I have been apologizing? I hadn't had that much time.

"Let's do it now," the duchess said, tossing her head like she was the queen of England. "We can split up the houses."

"It's almost dinnertime."

"That's when the people will be at home."

"And you'll annoy them because they want to make dinner."

"All right," Verity said. "I'll do it on my way home. I'll tell you tomorrow what I find out. And I'll bring Danny."

She got up and hoisted that bulging backpack to her shoulders.

"Thanks, Grandpa," she said, and started out the door.

"Wait," I said, getting up. "I'm coming."

Seven

On our way to the burned church's neighborhood we saw the Lutheran minister leaving his gray stone church on Hickory, the main street in town.

Hawley Thumper was a small man, short, thin, and gentle in manner. The word around town was Reverend Thumper liked people to live perfect lives in the church. He was, of course, often disappointed. I often wondered if he was perfect himself.

"Hello, Reverend Thumper," I said when we got close enough to get his attention.

"Oh, hello, Fatzinger," he said. "And is that Verity? How are you my dear?"

"I'm fine," Verity said.

"Good, good. Terrible fire last night, wasn't it?"

"Terrible," I said. "Do you know anything? See anything suspicious?"

He rubbed his small hands together as though he were warming them—but it was a warm September day. "Oh, dear, no," he said. "I understand it started inside the church, so of course I wouldn't have seen that. I've never set foot in there."

"Why is that, Reverend?"

"Well, I have my own flock to attend to."

"I understand they have different beliefs?"

"Well, we have differing approaches to theology," he looked at Verity, "you know, different ideas about religion. I wish them no harm. I will call on the Reverend Ringer to express my condolences and offer my help."

"How are your beliefs different?" I asked.

"Well, we are perfectly content to follow the leader of the protestants, Martin Luther. He was the *first*, you know."

"And I suppose they think they have refined—improved—on your earlier approach?"

"Well, I'm here to tell you Lutheranism needs no improving."

"Are you sorry for what happened across the street?" I nodded my head across the side street and one block up where we had a good view of the burned out church.

"Well, of course I'm sorry. Of course. Devastated that someone in this town should have such a mean spirit. In fact, I'm taking up a special collection to help rebuild the church."

"That's very nice. How much do you think you will raise?"

"Can't tell. We do have so many needs of our own that we struggle to meet every day. Sometimes we can get almost a thousand on special collections, sometimes only fifty."

Either way, I didn't see that going a long way toward rebuilding the church. Perhaps it was the thought that counted.

"Do you have any theories—ideas—who might have done this thing?" I waved my hand at the black, burned church.

"Oh, my, no. I just can't imagine it. Now, if you'll excuse me, I have to hurry to an appointment," and he bounded off down Hickory Street on which his church stood.

The duchess and I made our way up to the Reverend Ringer's burned-out church. It was on the corner, and we walked around it to see what the neighbors might have seen.

"It looks like the entry to the basement is on the side there," I said, pointing to concrete stairs that went down from ground level.

"Can you get into the church from the house?" the duchess asked.

"Let's look." We went back to Fifth Street. I couldn't tell from outside, and I didn't remember seeing any doors, but a wall of the house was shared with the church.

"I can ask Reverend Ringer," I said.

"Now?"

"Okay." We went to the door and rang the bell. Mrs. Ringer answered. "Oh, hello, Mr. Fatzinger. Have you found anything out?" She looked down at the duchess. "Hello, Verity."

"Hello," Verity said.

"I'm just starting," I said, though I thought that should be obvious. It was only this morning that she was cleaning to beat the band while I tried to talk to her husband.

"Is the reverend in?"

"Oh, no, he's...out."

"Well, perhaps you can help us. Is there a way

to get into the church from the house without going outside?"

"Well, yes, but not now. The church is gone."

"How did you do it—get into the church from here?"

"If you want to come in, I'll show you." We stepped inside, and she led us to the back of the house and showed us a door from the kitchen pantry.

"I can't open it," she said. "It was nailed shut for our security."

"Where's Danny?" Verity asked.

"Oh, he's off with his father."

"Baseball game?" I pried, since she apparently didn't want to tell.

"Oh, no," she said. "It's more of a..." she stopped, apparently changing her mind.

"Is he at the doctor again?" the duchess asked.

"Well, something like that. Yes, a doctor. That's it."

"I suppose the church had a custodian?" I asked.

"Well, yes, we still do, though he certainly doesn't have much of anything to do now that we've had a fire. Sterling suggested we utilize him to clean the house, but I wouldn't hear of it. That's my department."

"Yes, and you do a perfectly wonderful job of it," I said. I was going to add, 'I'll say that,' like her husband said all the time, but I didn't think she would find it funny.

"What's the custodian's name?"

"First of all we call him a sexton in our congre-

35

gation. His name is Casper Schultz."

"Like the ghost," the duchess said.

"Yes—just like the friendly ghost."

"Where does he live?"

"Why, just around the corner, next to the church—where the church was. We are like bookends—Casper on one side and the Reverend, Danny and me on the other. If you recall, he put us up the night of the fire."

"I take it he had his own key to the church?"

"Yes," she said, "but we never locked anything. Sterling used to fuss about churches that locked their doors—'locking out the people from God.'" She shook her head and clucked her tongue. "Not a good idea at all. The Lutherans down the block lock their doors all the time."

"You think if you'd locked your doors the church would not have been burned?"

"Well, I declare, there's just no telling about that, is there? You can't turn back the clock. We've wondered about it, though, I'll tell *you*. Plus we've taken to locking our own doors now."

"So anyone could have gotten into the church basement from anywhere?"

"I suppose that's correct."

"The main door of the church on this street?" I said pointing out to Fifth Street.

She nodded.

"Or down the steps into the basement from the side street?"

"Yes, that's so."

"Or even from your house?"

"Oh, but no one from here burned the church down."

I looked at Verity as if to say, I told you so. She didn't look at me.

"Were you at home when the fire started?"

"Yes. We had just finished dinner. The reverend was watching TV in the living room, Danny was upstairs doing his homework, and I smelled smoke. At first I thought it was left over from our dinner or a neighbor's building. I don't know how long after that I heard a siren, and we got a call from the sexton—Mr. Schultz you know—who told us the church was on fire. Well, you'd think we'd have been the first to know, living right next to it, but you see when you look out the front window you don't see the church at all. So we were like a horse with blinders.

"Sterling took the call from the sexton and we dashed right out of the house to watch the flames and see the firemen rushing to put it out, but I'm afraid it was too late."

Then I heard a car drive up. I looked out and saw Reverend Ringer and Danny get out of the car and walk up the four steps to the porch.

When the reverend took in the scene, his eyes passing over mine, then his wife's back to mine, his broad, generous smile evaporated from his face.

"What are you doing here, Fatzinger?" he asked, not too friendly.

"Came to ask you a few questions. We're working on your case."

I tried to check out Danny's expression, but I couldn't get a good look at him without being obvious.

"What did you want to ask me? It's nearly dinnertime—shouldn't you be in the kitchen, dear?" he said to his wife. I was getting a bad feeling.

She said, "Well, I didn't want to be rude to Mr. Fatzinger and Verity—they're trying to help."

"So what are your questions?" Sterling Ringer zeroed in on me with his laser-like eyes.

"Oh, your good wife answered them. We'll be on our way."

"You should confine your questions to me, if you don't mind."

"Oh, I don't mind at all. Next time I have questions I'll be sure and direct them to you. Have a nice evening."

Danny was trying to get the duchess's attention. I suspect he wanted to know if he could help. She said, "I'll talk to you tomorrow," and we left.

Eight

"Phew!" I said when we were back on the sidewalk. "I don't think we made the reverend very happy."

"No. He's not a happy person," said the duchess.

"What makes you say that? He has a wonderful smile. He *looks* happy."

"Danny says he is uptight."

"I suppose we would be too if our church burned down."

"Danny says he's always uptight."

"Let's check out that stairway to the basement again," I said, and we rounded the corner and stood at the top of the stairs, which were halfway back to the end of the church. I looked around to see who could see the top of the steps from their houses. The sexton who lived right next door had the only full view of it. There was a house across the street from which someone might have been able to see most of the concrete landing. From the house next to that someone could only see something if he went to or from the sidewalk at the street.

We checked the sexton's backyard. All the yards were open—no fences—as far as you could see. So I said to the duchess, "Anyone could come through these backyards without being seen across the street."

"But the people in these houses could see them. Someone could cut through any of these yards and come out on the next street. We better ask all the neighbors if they saw anything."

I noticed old Minnie Werner on her porch swing. "I don't think she ever leaves her front porch."

"She couldn't stay there all the time," the duchess corrected me. She was always very literal.

We crossed the street and went up to the porch. "Top of the day to you, Miz Werner," I said.

"Well, Bones," she said, fanning herself with a Ritter Funeral Parlor fan, "it's a hot one, ain't?"

"That it is," I said, "that it is. Some fire, huh?"

"It was that," she said, shaking her head and adding a tsk-tsk sound.

"Didn't happen to see anything strange going on over there before the fire?"

"Bones, you know I mind my own business. I don't pay any attention to the comings and goings of that place. I'm a Lutheran anyway, so it makes no difference to me what they do."

"I surely understand that, Miz Werner, I just thought you might have happened to see something— purely by accident, you understand."

"Well, if I ever *did* see anything it would be by accident, that's for sure—then I wouldn't pay no mind to it because I mind my own business."

"Of course you do, Miz Werner—of course you do. So, I suppose there was nothing unusual about last night."

She looked at me as though she thought I was

trying to trick her.

"I didn't see nothing..." she said, but her sentence didn't seem to end, and I had the feeling more was coming—then it came. "...'Cept that sexton staying in the church longer than usual."

"What time did he leave the church?"

"After eight. It was getting on to dark."

"What time does he usually leave?"

"Six on the dot. Why I swear that man would rather roast in the hot place than give God Almighty an extra minute of his time," she paused. A thought occurred to her. "That's since he started working days."

"When was that?" I asked.

"Couple weeks now, I expect."

"See anybody else around the church that night?"

"Nobody else."

"You go in the house for dinner?"

"Course I did," she said with a harrumph— "You don't think I maintain this size by fasting."

"What time was that?"

"Six—well, a little after. I usually set my watch by when Schultz—that's the sexton—comes up the stairs and goes in his house."

I turned to see what you could see from her porch—only a sliver of the step. "Did he go in the front or back?"

"Front—always goes in the front door—told me once he had to go in the back basement door of the church, but he could surely go in his own front door."

"But could he go in or out the back—if he wanted to—without you seeing him?"

"You see that line," she said, pointing across the street, "that space between his house and the church? He can't get anywhere without crossing that line—that's for sure."

"So what time did you go in the house last night?"

"When I didn't see hide nor hair of Schultzie, I began to worry. I almost called the church to see he was all right."

"Why didn't you?"

"Because I don't stick my nose in other people's business."

"So how long did you wait to go in your house?"

"'Bout fifteen minutes. I looked at the clock when I got there."

"Were you inside when you saw Mr. Schultz go into his house around eight?"

"No, I go back out after supper."

"What time was that last night?"

"Little before seven."

"So you were off duty, so to speak, from six-fifteen to seven or so."

"What you mean off duty?" she snapped. "I don't have any *duty* here. I just like the fresh air is all. I don't care a fig for what my neighbors are doing, if that's what you mean."

"Oh, no, not at all. Sorry," I said. "You friendly with Mr. Schultz?" I asked.

"I pass the time of day with him if I see him."

"Every night at six?"

She nodded. "He'll say—'Good evening, Miz Werner,' and I'll say, 'Lovely evening,' or something. If anyone has to say something different it's going to be me. You know, 'Good evening, Miz Werner,' 'Good evening, Mr. Schultz,' gets old, so I try to spice it up with a bit of a change."

"Good for you," I said. "Do you see him go in in the morning?"

"Oh, yes, I'm out here bright and early by seven. Schultz goes in about eight. Understand my being on the porch all day has nothing to do with any interest in anybody's business—I just want to make that perfectly clear."

"No, of course not," I said. I wanted to add, perish the thought, but I didn't think that would be appreciated.

The duchess was looking up and down the street—everywhere but at Miz Werner.

"Well, I'm much obliged to you, Miz Werner."

"For what? You come here looking for news, and I don't have any. I mind my own business."

I looked at Minnie Werner to see if there was a smile breaking out anywhere on her face, her mouth, her eyes—but no. She was dead serious.

"Good day to you, Miz Werner."

"And it has been that," she said. "Unlike yesterday."

The duchess and I moseyed to the corner, then turned it. We stood by the front steps of the church.

"Notice Minnie Werner can't see the front entrance to the church," I said. "Someone could have gone in here—making believe they were going to pray or something—and could have slipped down to the basement, started the fire and left the church."

Across the street was a double house—one half was a dentist's office, so there was probably no one there at dinner time.

"Shall we check across the street?" I asked the duchess. "See if anyone saw anything out front?"

"I can do it," she said. "You can go talk to the sexton."

"I'm not sure your mother would like you going into people's houses."

"Why not? I won't steal anything."

"Okay, you could just ask them all if they saw anything unusual that night. If they did, tell them I'll talk to them about it. But only on one condition."

"What?"

"You don't go in the house. Stay on the porch. I'll be at the sexton's on the other side of the church if you need me."

"All right," she said, and we went our separate ways.

Nine

I held back to watch the duchess at her first door. She did just what I asked—the woman held the screen door open for her to come in, but Verity declined. She was good at following directions.

I went back to Casper Schultz's house and rang the bell.

There was no answer. I rang three times, then went around to the back of the house—he wasn't there. I came back out front and looked across the street to where the big bulk of Minnie Werner was quietly swinging on her porch swing.

"He's in there," she said. "He just don't answer the door."

I went back to the front door. I tried the door. It was locked. I put my ear to the door. I couldn't hear anything.

The duchess was across Fifth Street at her second door. I noticed she didn't have anything to take notes on—she'd left her backpack at the Broad Street. Then I remembered what a phenomenal memory she had. She would be able to repeat what everyone said to her word-for-word.

I went back to the sexton's house. Instead of ringing the doorbell at the front door I walked around to the back, where I peered in the open window through the screen at the back door.

Schultz was sitting at his kitchen table, glaring back at me. "Go away," he said. "I don't want to talk to no reporters."

"I'm not a reporter," I said through the screen.

The sexton was short and spry. What little hair he had on his head was cut close to the bone. He sat at his table, hunched over as though waiting to pounce on anyone who tried to steal his food.

"I don't want to talk to nobody," he said.

"Sooner or later you're going to have to."

"I already talked to the cops. That was more than enough for me. You a cop?"

"I used to be. Now I work privately."

"Privately…? For who?"

"That would be private," I said.

"It's old Ringer, isn't it? He wants to hang this thing on me, and since I didn't do it the cops won't hang it on me. So he wants you to do it. Hey, wait a minute—aren't you Bones? Bones Fatzinger? I heard tell of you. You got a raw deal."

"Good of you to think so," I said. "How about letting me in so your neighbors don't have to hear everything we say?"

He considered that a moment, then said, "The door's open."

I tried it. It *was* open. I went in and joined him at his kitchen table. It looked like he was just finishing his supper, which seemed to be a peanut butter and jelly sandwich and a soda. Clara Rudy at the Broad Street would probably faint if she saw what he was eating. Not only were Clara's meals a lot heartier, they were healthier.

"So," I began, "I'm Bones Fatzinger and you're Casper Schultz—have I got that right so far?"

"Reckon you have."

"How long have you been the custodian at the church?"

"Never been."

"What? You aren't the janitor?"

"Nope."

"I thought…isn't this the janitor's house?"

"Calls me a sexton there. Old word. Means the same."

"Oh, yes…I heard…"

"You just cleans up after the pigs—don't matter how they call it."

"Pigs?"

"That's what I calls 'em—pigs. Way they throw stuff around thinking, 'Oh, they'll be someone else to pick up after me, someone not as good as me.' So I calls 'em pigs!"

"You call them pigs, and they call you sexton. I think sexton is better."

"Puttin' on airs, you ask me for my opinion—sexton!" He said it with a twist of his lips that made him look like an unhappy clown in the circus.

"Well, I'll call you whatever you like. What do you favor?"

"Don't make no never mind to me."

"Sexton does have a nice sound to it. Like the guy in those old novels who rang the church bells."

"We don't have church bells. The Lutherans

would drown us out."

"Okay—I'll call you Mr. Schultz."

He wrinkled his nose. "Casper's okay with me. I don't need no misters."

"When did you first see the fire?"

"After my supper."

"What time was that?"

"I have my supper when I gets home from work. That's usually around six. I don't make any fuss or anything. I usually just heat something up from the freezer—TV dinners and the like."

"Last night you had supper at six?"

"Last night I was later."

"How much later?"

"Maybe a half hour."

"How come?"

"I got this busybody across the street, and she watches my every move—she sees me into my house at night and out in the morning. Creeps me out. She's *always* there. Spooky. So last night I got it in my head to fools her. There was this cellar window—I could see her settin' on her porch swing, and she couldn't see me 'cause of the bush in front, but I could see through it—so I just waited till she went in for dinner afore I went to my house—through the *back* door. Other times I use the front. If I can't use the front door in the church at least I can in my own house. I have to walk a sight more to go in the front, but it's worth it."

"So how long was it till Minnie Werner went in?"

"'Bout fifteen minutes—but it was aggravating

her, I could see that, an' I just got the biggest kick out of it. What time she say I come home?"

"'Round eight."

He whooped it up at that. "Caught her good this time," he said.

"Maybe not so good if she swears you were in the church till eight. The fingers will point to you for starting the fire."

"I never did no such thing," he said. "I was going to burn something down it wouldn't be the church. Burn my job? That would be crazy."

"What *would* you burn?"

"I might go for the reverend's house."

"Don't get along?"

"I get along with everybody."

"Some better than others, no doubt."

"No doubt."

"How is the Reverend Ringer to work for?"

"Tough," was all he said.

"How tough?"

"Very."

"I mean in what way?"

"There's no pleasing him. He's always looking over my shoulder."

"Like Minnie Werner?"

"Exactly! 'Ceptin' he does pay me—not a lot, you understand, but I get the house and a few coins for my frozen dinners."

"So how did you discover the fire?"

"I thought I saw smoke. I wasn't sure it wasn't a big dust storm—so I goes to check it out, and I was not down the back steps half way before I feel this hot air like a furnace is blasting me. I saw some flames through the window in the door and high tailed it to the telephone to call the firemen."

"What time was that?"

"Somewhere around eight."

"Did you go to the front door of your house or the back that time?"

"Front."

"Why?"

"Habit, I guess. Panic. I wasn't thinking or I'd a gone in the back—it's closer."

"Any idea who started it?"

"No."

"Did you see anybody in the church between six and eight?"

"No—I can't see in the church from my house."

"Know anybody didn't like the church enough to burn it down?"

"No."

"Anybody dislike Reverend Ringer enough to burn his church?"

"Not besides me. Oh, I don't say he doesn't have some enemies, but like I said, you want to get him, burn his house—shouldn't be burning a house of God no how."

"How about the Reverend Ringer's boy?"

"Danny? What about him?"

"He get along with his dad?"

"What boy that age get along with his father?"

"Their relationship is no worse than the usual?"

"I don't know 'bout their personal affairs. I

50

don't expect the reverend is the model father, but I don't peg Danny for the model son either."

"Well, thanks, Casper—if you think of anything that might help, give me a call at the Broad Street, will you?"

"Sure thing."

I left his house to look for the duchess. Minnie Werner was sitting on her porch swing, fanning herself with the funeral home fan.

Ten

Outside, I quickly moved to the corner and down Fifth Street to catch up with the duchess before Miz Werner could call me back to gossip with her. I knew she was itching to find out what Schultz had told me.

I met the duchess as she was coming back up the street from her last door.

"What did you find out?"

"Nobody saw anything."

"Were any of them looking out their windows at the church?"

"No."

"Did everyone answer the door?"

"All but one. That one there," she pointed to the double house down from the dentist's office. "And the dentist."

"I'll talk to him tomorrow," I said. "I don't think he is in the front often. That's the waiting room." I knew that because he was *my* dentist.

We walked together back to the Broad Street Hotel so she could pick up her backpack and mosey on home.

"Are you going to bring Danny tomorrow after school?"

"He wants to come."

"What do you think?"

"It's okay."

"But you said you thought he did it."

"I know he did it."

"Did he confess to you?"

"No, he didn't have to. I know it."

"Then I don't see what good it would do to have him help investigate. He certainly isn't going to trap himself."

"We're only doing this because you don't believe me that Danny did it."

"What would you have me do? Take Danny to the police? What evidence do we have? I can't just show up at the police station and say, 'Arrest Danny Ringer for setting the fire.' They'll say, 'How do you know?' and I'll say, 'The duchess says so. That's good enough for me, and it ought to be good enough for you, too!'"

"You can tell the police we checked the neighborhood and nobody saw anybody go into the church, so it had to be someone who could go into the church and back out without going outside."

"Reverend Ringer? Mrs. Ringer? Mr. Schultz the sexton? He goes in and out all day long."

"Danny did it," she said. She had a stubborn streak, and it was not unusual for her to insist something was true when it wasn't.

"Besides," I said, "we have a watchdog on the side street—checking the cellar entry, because she can't see the front."

"Nobody saw anyone at the front."

"But no one was looking all day," I said. "Even

Miz Werner was in her house around the time the fire must have started."

The duchess didn't look convinced.

We got to the hotel. The duchess picked up her backpack, put her arms through the straps and said, "Tomorrow I'll bring Danny."

That night we had a Pennsylvania Dutch pot pie for dinner. Chicken, potatoes and homemade noodles in chicken broth—celery and onions too. Clara was a great cook.

After dinner I wrote down everything we knew about the case, and it wasn't much.

The next morning I called Doctor Trumbar, my dentist, whose office was across from the church. He said he'd be glad to talk to me at lunchtime.

I went early to knock on the door of the house where the duchess said no one was home. Still no answer—which gave me some extra time. First I crossed the street and walked through the fire damage of the church. I saw the steps to the basement and the steps up the front on Fifth Street, and the wide space where the two burned out doors had been. The door to the Ringer's house was nailed shut in the hope of making the family more secure.

I went back to the dentist's office and sat in the waiting room to wait for Doctor Trumbar. I looked out the window and tried to imagine someone going up those steps into the open church, slipping down to the basement, and lighting gasoline soaked rags and putting them under the wooden stairs—then going back up and out into the street, probably to return to watch the fire from somewhere.

But who, and why?

Doctor Trumbar came out as soon as his patient left and greeted me in his easy, friendly manner. All the dentists I knew were friendly, easy-going people: nice. I suspect it is because they have to make up for the fear people have of going to the dentist. I mean, it wouldn't do if they were quiet and reserved like undertakers.

We walked to the corner, where there was a tea shop in an old, landmark house. There we had little sandwiches at little tables with a lot of little old ladies. This was not a macho, he-man place, but Carl Trumbar was always watching his waistline.

We got our plates of cute little sandwiches, and I made a mental note to hurry to the Broad Street Ice Cream Parlor to have Clint make me one of his fabulous banana splits for dessert. Like Minnie Werner said from her porch swing, "You can't maintain this bulk by fasting."

"Know anything about the fire across the street from your office?"

"Nothing," he said, taking a bite of a cucumber and cream cheese sandwich. "Came up with all my patients of course, and none of them know anything either. No scuttlebutt, no rumors—everyone is in the dark."

"Motives?"

"Oh, I don't know. That reverend is a strange one, though. All smiles and self-righteousness. Came here from the coal regions, I believe. I went to welcome him into the neighborhood—he was so smiley I thought he must be a dentist. He gave me a lot of God and Jesus talk, but I guess that's what you do when you're in that line of work. Now I never thought of talking fillings and extractions to him—it was just a friendly, good neighbor call. I just never got a good feeling about him. I see him on the street once in a while and at the Rotary Club up at Clint's Broad Street Hotel, but I just never felt relaxed around him.

"Now, you take Reverend Fowler up at the Baptist Church—he plays poker with us every Wednesday. Never misses. He has someone dying, they have two choices—wait until his game is over or go ahead and die without him. A real regular guy, one of the fellas, you know?"

"Yeah."

"Now, you take Reverend Ringer across the street. Isn't anybody in this town going to invite him to play cards. Why, I bet it's against his religion."

"Think he'd burn down his own church?"

"Oh, that might be a little far fetched."

"How about his son Danny?"

"The boy? Burn down his father's church? Now you're really talking far fetched." He thought a minute, munching on a tuna salad sandwich on a little round piece of rye bread. "Coming to think of it, I hear the father and boy don't get along." He took a sip of his tea (what can you expect at a tea shop?) then said, "Nah, the kid is only, what? Ten years old?" he said.

"Twelve," I corrected him.

"Yeah, well, whatever, I just don't think it's in the cards."

Eleven

I saw the duchess coming down Broad Street toward
the hotel with this funny looking guy, who had trouble walking in a straight line—either that or he was
dancing to avoid the cracks in the sidewalk. They
made quite a pair: the duchess with her head held
high, walking as though on a straight chalk line and
this dancing monkey zigzagging back and forth on the
sidewalk.

I was rocking on a rocking chair on the
porch—the rocking motion helped me to think—and
what I thought was that having Danny Ringer "help"
us was a bad idea. Just looking at him put me in mind
of that wonderful but scary expression: a loose can-
non.

When they got to the steps of the front porch
the duchess took them methodically, one at a time.

Danny Ringer bounced up two, then back
one—he couldn't stop dancing.

The duchess sat in the rocker next to me without taking her backpack off. She did this most of the
time, and it drove me nuts.

The boy danced from one foot to the other. He
had curly red hair and freckles and was not as tall as
the duchess. He was chewing bubble gum and seemed

to take delight in blowing the biggest bubbles imaginable. From time to time he stuck his fingers in his mouth and got a hold of some of the gum and pulled it out of his mouth on a long string.

"You must be Danny?" I said, since the duchess did not seem to be about to introduce us.

"That's me," he said, blowing a wizard-sized bubble.

"I understand you want to help us find the person who burned your father's church."

"Yup."

"Why?"

"Dunno," he said, skipping from foot to foot in front of my rocking chair, "just do."

"But what can you help with?"

"I know the layout of the place."

"Yes?"

He shrugged.

"Okay," I said, "maybe you can help. How do you get along with your father?"

"I don't know my father."

"What? Reverend Ringer is not your father?"

"I'm adopted."

I looked at the duchess. I couldn't tell from her stone face if she'd known that or not. "How old were you?"

"Just a baby. I don't remember anything."

"When did they tell you?"

"As long as I can remember. Whenever I do anything wrong the old man says, 'What do you expect? He's adopted.'"

"The old man?"

"Yeah."

"You call Reverend Ringer the old man?"

"Yeah, I don't like to call him Dad, because he's not."

"Hmm, do I gather you don't care for him very much?"

"That's right on the money, Pops."

"Pops?"

"You got it."

"So a guy who calls me 'Pops' and his father 'the old man' might be angry enough to burn down the old man's church?"

"Why would I do that?" he asked. "Unless he was in it, then it might be a good idea. But he wasn't in it."

"Okay—who would want to burn the church without him in it? Any ideas—people who don't like him?"

"Nobody likes him."

"Oh, Danny, that may be a little strong," I said. "People come to his church."

"Well, I don't know any of them," he grumbled.

"So, how about giving me some names?" I asked.

"Start with the sexton—Casper."

"Mr. Schultz?"

"I call him Casper—like the ghost—he's like a ghost, creeping around the church all day making believe he's working."

"Wait," I said, "let me guess. Casper Schultz caught you smoking in the boiler room—that's why you say he creeps around."

Danny looked at me with such surprise that he stopped dancing *and* chewing his bubble gum all at once. We said nothing for a while—I thought the duchess might break the silence, but no such luck. Then just as suddenly as he stopped, Danny started again—the bouncy dance, the heavy chomping of the bubble gum.

"The old man got Casper good, this time."

"What'd he do?" I asked.

"Casper used to work nights, but the old man thought he was doping off—wasn't doing anything, so he told him he had to work days."

"When did that happen?"

"A couple weeks ago, I guess."

"Was that after Mr. Schultz told your father—or excuse me—the old man—he caught you smoking in the basement?"

"That's not true," he said, but I didn't believe him.

"So you think Casper Schultz, the church sexton, burned down his work place?"

"Yeah."

"And how do you think he figures to make a living without a place to work?"

I could see from Danny's face he hadn't thought about that.

"Any ideas how to prove the sexton burned the church?"

"You're the detective."

"But I thought you wanted to help."

"I do want to help. Tell me what I can do."

"I told you—give me the names of anybody

that dislikes your father so much they'd risk going to jail by burning down his church."

"Jail?" he asked, as though that was something he hadn't considered. "They could make it look like an accident."

"They didn't. The firemen are sure it was set on purpose, and they know where."

"Where?"

I looked him over closely to see if he really didn't know. I couldn't tell. "You tell me," I said.

"Well, I don't know. How do you expect me to know?"

"Maybe your father told your mother, and you heard it."

"He's not my father!"

"Maybe you heard it from someone else."

"Who?"

"And maybe you know because you did it yourself."

"Why would I want to help find out who did it if I did? I'd already know."

I looked at the kid. I couldn't tell for sure if he was telling the truth or not. My first thought was not to let him help. Then I thought, if he did do it—start the fire that burned his father's church (I would insist on calling him his father no matter what he said)—he probably would slip up, and we could catch him in a big mistake that would prove he did it.

More important, it would be like having a spy in the enemy camp—we could get information from the inside that the police probably wouldn't get.

"Okay, Danny," I said. "I'll let you help under

some conditions."

"What?"

"First, you don't tell anyone you're helping. Can you come here after school with Verity?"

"Except when the old man takes me to the shrink."

"Shrink? Psychiatrist? What for?"

"He thinks I'm nuts."

"Are you?"

"He's the one who's nuts."

"What does the shrink say?"

"Nothing. He just asks me all these stupid questions."

"Do you answer them?"

"Sometimes."

"Did he ask you if you burned the church?"

"Yeah."

"What did you say?"

"No—the old man put him up to it."

"So your father thinks you might have done it?"

"He thinks everybody could have done it. And he's *not* my father."

"That's another condition."

"What?"

"I'm going to call him your father, because that's really what he is. You may think what you want, but he took you from some folks who gave you up because they couldn't handle you, were too poor, or whatever. He fed you, clothed you, raised you as best he knew and as far as I'm concerned, he's your father."

Danny considered this. The gum chewing

slowed, and his head bobbed up and down rhythmically as his feet stopped their shuffling dance.

"You sound just like him," he said, but I could see that the idea coming from someone else made him consider it differently.

"Well, if you can't come here, and you have any news that might help our investigation, you can give it to Verity. She's going to be my assistant on the case."

"Can I be your assistant too?"

"You accept my conditions?"

"I guess so," he said, looking like it was a big compromise for him.

"Okay. Keep your ears open around the house. You can listen to your father's calls since he can't shut the door of his church study. Where does he work in the house?"

"He calls from the kitchen."

"Can you hang around so you can hear?"

"When I'm not in school."

"Weekends?"

"Yeah."

"Tell us everything he says about the fire."

"Okay."

Clint came out on the porch. "What are you all doing out here? Wouldn't you like a taste of ice cream?"

We all jumped at the chance and followed him into the ice cream and soda fountain for banana splits on the house.

Twelve

I was having breakfast with Clara and two other guests when Clint came into the dining room to tell me there was a telephone call for me.

I took it in the soda fountain so I wouldn't disturb the guests' breakfast.

It was the Reverend Ringer. He sounded unhappy. "Fatzinger," he called me, "I want to meet with you now. Come to the library park. I'm leaving in five minutes, I expect to see you when I get there."

He had almost the same distance to go as I did. I didn't like his tone. I wasn't a slave, and I expected to be treated with more consideration.

My breakfast was half finished and getting cold, and I was still hungry. He expected to see me when he got there, he said. But what would happen if he didn't see me? If I came a little late? Just give me time to finish my breakfast? Would he fire me? Would he be able to find someone else to take gruff orders from him?

I decided to finish my breakfast, and I didn't rush. No sense getting indigestion over it.

The library was about a mile from the Broad Street, and it was a lovely day. So I decided to walk. The Reverend Ringer would drive, I was sure; but when he blew up at me for taking so long I'd just say, "Oh you drove? I thought you were walking. Such a short way to drive, especially when we are supposed to be saving gasoline."

He could rant and rave, but he couldn't do much else.

When I got there, there was no sign of Reverend Ringer. I decided he had come, not found me, and left in a huff of anger. Just to be sure I went inside and asked the librarian if he had been there. She said, if he had been there, he hadn't come in.

Our library was such a pleasant place, I roamed around the shelves and stopped short when I came to the Child Psychology section. I saw several books that seemed like they could tell me something about the reverend's psychology with his son.

I took the books to a reading table near the front door, so I could see out the window if the reverend came. In the books I found sections on the attitudes of preteens and how to cope with them; rebellion; the special strains of father/son relationships; how to tell your child he's adopted. ("Most parents don't have any say in what kind of child they get—we picked you.") That was a long way from how the reverend handled the issue with his son Danny.

I was so caught up in the books that I didn't see the reverend come into the library. He stood over me, looking down at my books and frowning.

"What are you reading, Fatzinger?" Well, I knew he knew what I was reading, because he was looking at the books, so I didn't answer. I just closed the books I had open so he could see the covers if he wanted to.

"Special Strains of Father/Son Relationships," he read aloud. "I didn't know you had a son, Fatzinger."

I started to tell him I didn't, but caught myself. We both knew I didn't have any children.

"I thought you were going to meet me outside," he said.

"I was outside," I said. "You weren't there. Five minutes, you said. It's been a lot longer, so I came in here to pass the time."

"On psychology. Yes—well we don't need any more of that. We're doing the whole psychiatry bit. Let's go outside."

I slipped the books on the counter and put my library card on top. "I'll be back for these," I said and followed the leader out the door onto the beautiful grass looking a lush deep green in the gleaming sun. The reverend led me to a bench and sat.

"Sit," he said, as I imagined he would say to a puppy dog. So I sat next to him on the bench with our backs to Main Street going to Allenville, the closest big city.

"Fatzinger, I've been hearing some distressing things about you."

Distressing? I was surprised to hear him say that. "What's bothering you?"

"What's bothering me is the way you are running roughshod over the neighborhood asking all kinds of questions about me and my family. You have been hired to find the person who burned my church down, not to do a psychological profile on the reverend's family."

"I don't know what you mean. We have gone through the neighborhood—mainly that is, Verity has—to find out if anyone saw anything the night of the fire, any suspicious persons going in or out of the church."

"Did you find any?"

"Not yet. But who gave you the idea we were asking questions about your family?"

"I have my sources," he said.

"Well, I wish I knew who they were so I could straighten them out."

"You mean you haven't been trying to psycho-analyze the Ringers?"

So he was bluffing—imagining we were finding something out about him he probably didn't want found out. "No," I said.

"My main concern is for my boy Danny. He's adopted, you know, and his ego and psyche are very fragile. I wouldn't want that delicate balance disturbed in any way, you understand?"

I didn't answer, but looked at him curiously. Was he going to blame the boy's attitudes on me?

He went on, "I understand my boy Danny was at the Broad Street Hotel with you and Verity after school yesterday. He did not have my permission to go there, and I don't want him in that den of iniquity." The reverend was using a Bible phrase for an undesirable place, a place with bad people.

"What? An ice cream parlor and soda fountain?"

"No telling what sorts of persons hang out at a

place like that. I'll bet there's smoking and worse going on."

"No," I said. "Not at Clint Rudy's place."

"Well, what was Danny doing there?"

"What makes you think he was there?"

"One of my church members saw him and reported the incident to me."

"Incident? Like it was a crime for him to be in an ice cream parlor with a classmate?"

"We're a very strict denomination. Danny is an impressionable boy. He's adopted, you know." He said that as though that explained everything.

"Yes, you told me. Twice. And he told me. Do you think it's to the boy's benefit for you to say that so often?"

The reverend stiffened, his back shot up then back. "We're very honest in our family."

"Honesty can be good, Reverend, but in excess it can also be brutal."

"I was adopted," he said. "My father always said I was. It didn't hurt me."

That was debatable, I thought, but I didn't say anything.

"Perhaps Danny is not as strong as you are," I said.

"Nonsense. Then I'll make him as strong."

"Of course, it's not my business, but if I were you, I'd soft peddle the adoption talk. He knows it, he won't forget it, he doesn't need to be reminded all the time."

The reverend's back stiffened again. "Are you trying to tell me how to raise my boy?"

"Your son? Do you ever call him your son? Does he call you Father?"

"You are trying to meddle in my private affairs. Have you done anything else besides stirring up the neighbors?"

"We've had one day. If you aren't satisfied, I'll donate my time to date."

"No, no, I want answers. The fire department isn't really set up to solve the mystery. The police have other things on their minds. Keep at it."

"With your cooperation?"

"Certainly."

"Then tell me what your gut feelings are about it."

"I don't know."

"I think you have some idea."

"No, I…"

"Do you think Danny did it?"

The reverend froze on the bench. I could feel the ice in the September air. "Don't you say that to anybody. The boy was under our supervision all evening. He was in his room studying. He is so psychologically fragile I fear if anyone suggests this to him there's no telling what he might do. It isn't true, so let's not talk about it."

"The sexton?"

"Ah, Casper Schultz," the reverend said. "I wish I were less suspicious of him. He's a drinker. We shouldn't have a drinker on our staff. It creates many problems. I fear he doesn't like me. I had to change his schedule from nights to days because all he did at night was drink and fall asleep. His duties suffered terribly. So now he works days, under my close supervision."

"Would he burn down his place of employment?"

"Perhaps it was an accident, and he has to cover it up."

"Think so?"

"I don't know. This is all very sensitive. That's why I want you to report to me, and don't share you're findings with anyone else."

I bid Reverend Ringer goodbye and watched him get in his car and drive off up the street. Then I went inside and picked up my books. I thought I'd give them to Verity. She loved to read, and she never forgot anything she read.

Thirteen

I was on the porch after school when the duchess came down the sidewalk alone. When she got to the porch I asked, "Where's Danny?"

Verity hesitated before speaking as she usually did. "His father took him to the psychiatrist again."

"Didn't he just go?"

"Yes."

"What's up?"

"His father thinks you are a bad influence on Danny."

"Really?"

"That's what he says. I think his father knows Danny started the fire, but he doesn't want anyone else to know."

"The reverend told me Danny was in his room studying when the fire was started."

"He is wrong."

"But it's such a small house. How could anyone do anything without the others knowing?"

"Danny's father and mother were watching television, and they didn't notice Danny going through the door connected to the church, and they didn't see him come back. It didn't take long." The sing-song in her voice had an eerie quality to it—like she was this all-knowing, all-seeing, mysterious person.

"Well, it's a nice theory, but how are we going to prove it?"

"I'll prove it."

"Oh, you?" I said. Someone was getting too big for her britches again. "How?"

"It's a secret."

"Secret? A secret? That's not very helpful."

"You wouldn't understand."

"No? What would I have to do to understand?"

"You don't know anything about e-mail, do you?"

"No," I had to admit I didn't.

"See? So there."

"But you could teach me, couldn't you?"

"Do you have a computer?"

"No."

"So how can you learn about e-mail if you don't even have a computer?"

"Couldn't you show me on your computer?"

She seemed to consider this possibility. "I don't know about that," she said.

The duchess was infuriating me. Out of the goodness of my heart I let her help with the investigation, then before I knew it, it was like I was working for her.

"How long will Danny and his dad take at the psychiatrist?"

"An hour."

"Where is he?"

"In Allenville."

"Do you know what time his appointment is?"

"Four o'clock."

I looked at my watch. Ten of four. "I think I'll take this opportunity to talk to Grace Ringer. She seems freer to talk when her husband's not around."

"I'll go with you," the duchess said.

"Oh, no," I said. "This is going to be my secret. If we're going to have secrets, we both can have them."

One of the maddening things about the duchess was her face never seemed to show what she was thinking. It was like she had only one expression. She could be happy or sad, and her face was always the same.

"So I'll see you tomorrow after school," I said. "So long."

She got up and came with me.

"Hey," I said, "this is me alone. My secret."

She walked with me in silence until we crossed the bridge over the railroad. Then I said, "Duchess, no. You are not coming. This is an adult thing anyway. Mrs. Ringer will probably feel better about talking to an adult alone rather than having a child underfoot."

"Mrs. Ringer likes me."

"I'm sure she does, but that doesn't change my mind."

When we got to the stoplight, the only one in town, the duchess should have gone straight across the street to go home. I turned left to go to Mrs. Ringer's but Verity turned left with me.

"Verity! Verity, you can't come. Sorry."

She came anyway.

"Do you want to make a trade?" she said as we walked down Hickory Street to Fifth Street. Hickory was the busy main street that changed names at the triangle.

"What kind of trade?"

She didn't answer right away, and so we were within a block of the church and the reverend's home when she finally spoke up. I wondered if she'd done it purposely to stay with me until it was too late to keep her from going along. So I stopped dead on the sidewalk and said, "Okay, Duchess, what is it?"

"You let me come along to talk to Danny's mother, and I'll teach you how to use e-mail."

I shook my head. "Not good enough."

"Why not?"

"Because I want to know your secret. The one you said proves that Danny did it."

"Well, you'll know that after I teach you how to read e-mail."

I thought a moment, considering my choices. How good a deal was this? Her secret was probably nothing but a child's fantasy, but here she was sticking to me like glue, and what would I do if she simply followed me to the Ringer's door? Physically overpower her?

"When can you teach me the computer and e-mail?"

"Saturday."

"The day after tomorrow?"

"Yes."

"That okay with your mother?"

"Yes. You can ask her."

"Okay," I said. "Deal." I put out my hand and she shook it. I was pleased, as I knew physical contact and touch were not things that came easily to her.

So the two of us presented ourselves at the front door of the parsonage, the home of the Reverend and Mrs. Ringer and their son Danny.

Grace's voice sang out happily, "Come in," when she heard the bell. But when she opened the door her face fell with disappointment. "Oh, it's you," she said unhappily.

"How are you, Mrs. Ringer?" I asked.

"Oh, Grace. Call me Grace."

"Grace, may we come in a minute?"

"Well..." she said, not sure. "My husband would not like me to talk to you."

"But why not? He's hired me..." I looked at the duchess by my side, "us, to investigate the fire."

"I know."

"So we work for him, and you too. Both of you."

"He just doesn't like me getting involved in church things. It's like it's his business, and I am just the wife. It's okay for me to be in the front pew in church every Sunday and to be at the potlucks and the ladies' Bible study, but he really doesn't want me to express any personal opinions."

"Oh, pshaw," I said. "You're a person like anyone else. You have your ideas, your special knowledge, your opinions. Just let us come in to talk for a few minutes. Verity here is a friend of Danny, you know."

"I know," she said, looking up and down the

street as if to see if her husband had suddenly and surprisingly returned. "Well," she said, "only for a minute then."

She stood aside, and we stepped into her living room. It seemed even smaller than it had before.

"May I get you some tea and cookies?" she asked.

"No thanks," I said.

Grace looked at the duchess, and I was afraid she was going to ask for some refreshment and thereby cut our valued time. Mercifully, she said, "No, thank you."

"I...we were wondering, Grace, if you remember anything unusual about the evening leading up to the fire?"

"I don't really," she said. But she was so nervous about it, I didn't believe her.

"What were you doing before you heard the fire?"

"I was watching television."

"Where?"

"Right here in the living room."

"Where was your husband?"

"We were watching the news together. He always likes to watch the news."

"What do you like to watch?"

"Oh, it doesn't matter to me. News is fine."

And, I thought, if her husband wanted to watch boxing matches that would be fine too.

"Where was Danny?"

"Up in his room," she said, "Danny was studying, but I can't swear to that."

"What else does he do in his room?"

"Oh, he plays with his computer. He does all kinds of things on the internet. He's a whiz, really."

"Do you or your husband do computers?"

"Oh, goodness no. We're old fashioned. Danny wanted one when he was six years old, and I worked on the reverend for three years before he broke down and let him have it. Well, we both think he spends far too much time with it, but I guess it is better than a lot of the things a boy that age could do."

"Oh, yes indeed," I said. " Do you know what he does specifically with the computer?"

"Oh, we try not to interfere. There are a lot of games you can play, you can write letters to others and press a button and the letter goes to as many people as you want it to. E-mail I think they call it. Is that right dear?" she looked at the duchess.

"Yes."

"You have a computer, do you dear?"

"Yes."

"You take it to school, I hear."

"Yes."

"Do you play games with it?"

"Not in school I don't. My handwriting is hard to read sometimes, so I print my work out from the computer and everybody can read it, including me."

"Oh dear," Grace said, "how precious."

I looked at the TV set in the corner of the small living room, then at the chair Grace was sitting in. It was just behind the big reclining chair that was surely the master of the house's sole and separate property. The chairs' backs were facing the kitchen where the door into the church was.

"Did Danny ever go over to the church from the house for anything?"

"Oh, no. Danny didn't care much for the church or anything about it. He is a rebel, I guess. The reverend always said he was adopted." Then, as though I might not understand, she added, "He was so different from the reverend and me that he always wanted to add the adoption thing so people would understand that there was no genetic link. You know, he didn't share our genes."

"If you were watching television, do you think someone could come and go through that door off the kitchen and into the church?"

"Oh, goodness," Grace said, "who would want to do that?"

"So on the night of the fire, you weren't aware of anyone going back and forth to the church from the house?"

Her eyes moved from side to side, suspiciously; she even looked at the duchess as if pleading for help.

"No...I wasn't." But she was starting to think.

"Do you think your husband has any suspicion that Danny might have started the fire?"

"Oh, goodness no. They don't always get along as well as they could, twelve is a difficult age..." she looked at the duchess, "...for a boy," she clarified her statement. "But Danny would never do a thing like that. No, no, no. It just isn't like him."

From what I'd seen of Danny, I'd think it was very much like him.

"Now, Bones, I'm going to have to ask you to

go. The reverend and Danny will be back any minute, and he would not be happy to know I was talking to you."

I stood with the duchess. "Thanks for your help. Has there been any discussion in the house about the fire and who might have started it?"

"Please go," she said, not answering me. "I don't want any trouble."

Outside, the duchess said, "Danny did it."

"I wouldn't be surprised," I said, "But we have no proof."

"I have it," she said.

"What is it?" I asked.

"You'll see on Saturday."

Fourteen

While the duchess was in school with Danny on Friday, I went back to the neighborhood of the church to see if the person that the duchess missed when she went door to door was home.

I knocked at the door. A thin older woman opened the door. I thought she was frail and trying to look sprightly.

"I'm Bones Fatzinger," I introduced myself. "I'm looking into the fire across the street. I was wondering if you could answer a few questions?"

"Well, sure," she said. "It's about time someone came around. Want to come in?"

I did. "We tried the other day but no one answered the door."

"Oh, I was out in Macungie, attending to my sister. She's got the gout so bad."

The living room, almost a carbon copy of the Ringer house, was dark and full of little ceramic fig-urines of birds and animals. There was wallpaper with cabbage roses that I thought was there to make the room look more cheerful. I don't think it worked.

"Were you here the day of the fire…oh, I didn't get your name."

"Priscilla Keller," she said. "You can call me

Pris. Everybody does, although I ain't what you'd call prissy. And yes, I was here the day of the fire."

"See anything unusual?"

"Well, set yourself there on the couch, and I'll tell you."

I sat on the couch, she in a rocking chair facing me. She rocked as she talked with an energetic motion that almost made me dizzy.

"I didn't see anything unusual that day at the church, but then I don't set on my porch all day watching the world go by. No, I'm out doing things, you know?"

I knew.

"Now you take Miz Werner over there. She's one to tell you the comings and goings of everybody on the planet."

"Yes, I talked to her."

"She see anything?"

"Yes, but I'm not sure it will help."

"What'd she see?"

"Just movements of the sexton. I'm not sure how it connects."

"Well, it's the sexton I seen at the gas station the day of the fire."

"Oh?"

She nodded and sucked in her lips.

"I was gassing up my old jalopy. I swear that thing drinks gas like a man gone without water in the desert for forty days and forty nights."

"Was Casper Schultz getting gas for his car?"

"Don't have no car, least ways I know of."

"Oh? So what was he doing at the gas station?"

"Buying gas!" She said as though that was an astonishing thing to be doing at a gas station.

"But not for his car?"

She shook her head as she rocked so her body was going in two directions at once. "Had one of them there cans you carry gas out in."

"What did you think?"

"What's a man doesn't have a car need gasoline for? Mind you, I thought nothing of it at the time, but after the fire! Gets you thinking. Started with gasoline, I hear. Maybe someone should ask if there is any of that gas left."

"Are you a member of the church?"

"Yes, I am. And I can tell you there is plenty bad blood between the sexton and the reverend. They just do not get on at all."

"You think Casper Schultz would burn down the church to spite the reverend?"

"All's I know is what I saw at the gas station."

"Would he burn down his livelihood? That's what happened. If you don't have a church, you don't have a need for a sexton."

"Don't know nothing about that."

"How long have you belonged to the church?"

"Long's I can remember. Long before this here pastor came to town, and this here sexton."

"Are you happy at the church?"

"What kinda question's that?" she asked. "Do you go to church to get happy?"

"Well...I..."

"Nothing like it. Reverend Ringer tells us how we should live our lives, how to obtain heavenly salvation. Doing your duty may not give you a barrel of laughs, but that's just your duty."

"Like Reverend Ringer, do you?"

"Like? What do you mean like? He's the pastor, isn't he?"

"Yes," I said. "Take his side in a dispute with the sexton?"

"Well, certainly yes. He's the pastor!"

"Know anything about Danny, his son?"

"Well, I know he's his son. He's adopted, you know."

"Yes."

"Far's I know they get along. I see them go places together."

"Know where they go?"

"None of my business. I don't meddle."

"The Reverend Ringer took Danny to a psychiatrist," I said, and as soon as it was out of my mouth, I knew it was a mistake. I could see her running across the street to tell the reverend what I told her.

"Well, if that don't beat all..." she said and seemed to reach for a word that didn't come. "Why do you suppose he'd do that? Psychiatry is heathen. You have a problem, you take it to the Lord in prayer."

"Think Danny has a problem?"

"Yes well, I wouldn't know. I don't meddle."

"Thank you for talking to me," I said, standing up from the couch. "If you think of anything else that might help, you can call me at the Broad Street."

She didn't answer, nor did she get up. She seemed to be thinking over what I'd said. She seemed to be in a trance from the constant, serious rocking.

As I let myself out, I could still hear the clank clanking sound of the wooden chair rocking back and forth across the wood floor.

Clank, clank, clank, clank.

I crossed the street to talk to the sexton about what she had said. I found him in his backyard reading the paper.

"Hello there," I said with enthusiasm in my voice. "How are you doing today?"

He looked up from the paper. "Fair to middlin," he said. "Course, I'd rather be reading on my front porch, but I'd be under the watchful eyes of old lady Werner."

"I've just been across the street talking to Miz Keller, Priscilla Keller. You know her?"

"'Course I know her. Don't I know everybody that belongs to this church?"

"Says she saw you at the gas station the other day."

He thought a moment, then nodded. "Yes, I believe she did."

"You were getting a can of gas."

"That's right," he was looking at me suspiciously.

"Your car run out of gas?"

"Don't have a car."

"Oh?" I let a silence pass between us, hoping he would fill it with an explanation. He didn't.

"What you want a can of gas for if you don't have a car?"

He looked at me as though I'd just lost my marbles. "For the lawn mower," he said. "How you figure on making the lawn mower run if you don't have any gas?"

I must have blushed sixteen shades of red on that one. "Did you mow the lawn?" I said, looking around at the black burned grass around the church.

"What's it look like?" he asked.

"It looks burned. But did you get to mow it before it burned?"

"Saturday's my day to mow the grass. Reverend wants it looking perfect for Sunday services."

"Where's the gas can now?"

"Gone."

"Gone?"

He nodded, "Burned up in the fire."

"So we don't know if it was used to start the fire."

"I reckon it was," he said.

"How so?"

"I stored it in the equipment room right next to the stairs. Whoever started the fire didn't have to go far to get the fuel."

"Wasn't you?"

"Wasn't me."

Fifteen

The whole town of Ephesus was soupy with a foggy drizzle on Saturday when I walked across the railroad bridge, through the town triangle and up to the Buscador residence, a walk of perhaps fifteen minutes. It wasn't really rainy, but I had to wear my raincoat and hat to keep reasonably dry.

The duchess answered the door, and I followed her into the house, where I waved at her mother who was in her side room law office with a client.

I followed the duchess to the basement, which was set up like a rec room with a table soccer game, a TV, and the duchess' pride and joy, a computer.

She sat in front of the computer and pushed some buttons that were beyond my experience. I stood over her shoulder. She hadn't spoken to me since I arrived. The duchess was a young woman of few words.

Her manipulation of the keyboard brought to the screen a bunch of words that made no sense to me at all. They looked like no language I'd ever seen. She still said nothing.

"Okay, Duchess," I said. "What's the mystery here?"

She hesitated. "Read it," she said.

"It's gibberish," I said.

Pause. "Not if you read it right," she said.

I could see she was in the mood to tease me.

"Okay," I said. "How do you read it right?"

"Guess."

I looked at the letters.

YM REHTAF REVEN SLLAC EM NOS was the message.

PLEH EM I EVAH SUOIRES SMELBORP was another.

The third was I TSUM OD GNIHTEMOS NOOS RO I LLIW OG YZARC.

"Give me a hint," I said.

"The writer never signs his name."

"Or her…"

"His," she said firmly.

"All right," I said, "His. Are you talking about a connection to our case?"

"Yes."

"How do you know if he didn't sign his name?"

"I know," she said.

"Are you going to let me in on the secret?"

"I'll give you more hints. You don't know about e-mail, do you?"

"No," I had to admit I didn't.

"You have to have an e-mail address so some-one can write to you. They have to have your address."

"Okay," I said without adding, "So what?"

"This mystery person had my e-mail address."

"How did he get it?"

"I gave it to him."

"So it's not a mystery. You know who it is."

"Yes, I know, but he is trying to make believe I don't know."

"Why?"

"He's embarrassed."

"Is that why he's writing this gibberish?"

"It isn't gibberish to him."

"What is it? Nonsense?"

"He's dyslexic. He's making up a code."

"Oh," I said and looked back at the screen. I read the words backwards. "That's why he has so much trouble in school. Everything looks backwards to him."

MY...FATHER...NEVER...CALLS...ME...SON.

The next:

HELP...ME...I...HAVE...SERIOUS...PROBLEMS.

And the third:

I...MUST...DO...SOMETHING...SOON...OR...I...WILL...GO...CRAZY.

I looked at the duchess.

"Danny did it," she said.

"Can we prove he sent these?"

"They came from his e-mail address."

"What is it?"

"Myson@aol.com."

"Could anyone use that address?"

"If they knew the password to make it work."

"Even if we could prove Danny sent these, he doesn't really say he started the fire, does he?"

"Danny did it," she said again. Repetition of

words and phrases was a symptom of her disease.

"But suppose—just suppose now—the sexton got access to a computer and sent these messages to make it look like Danny was unstable—or disturbed. Make us think Danny did it, when it was actually the sexton—or maybe even someone else."

"Danny did it."

"And maybe Danny did do it, but Casper Schultz, the sexton, wants us to know it."

"Danny did it."

"So you say. Now we just need some proof."

"I'm going to get it," she said.

"How are you going to do that?"

"With e-mail."

"How?"

"I send e-mails to him too."

"May I see them?"

She stared straight ahead without answering.

"Duchess," I said, "Verity—"

"I just encourage him to tell me everything."

"And does he?"

"Not yet, but he will."

"Well, you're certainly an optimist. Let me see some of your e-mails to him."

"When he admits it, maybe then I'll show you."

It all sounded a little too good to be true to me. "Aren't you afraid he'll get caught?"

"No."

"Maybe we should just ask him. He might tell us."

"No, he wouldn't," she said. "He has to do it on his own."

"I could use some police tricks that I know."

"What kind of tricks? Torture?"

"No, no—I could say, 'Well, we've narrowed it down,' then pause and watch his face, then say, 'It's you.'"

"That won't work with Danny."

"Do you think his mother knows?"

"Everybody knows—his mother, his father, his psychiatrist. I know, and now you know."

"Not so fast," I said. "I don't know anything of the kind. And if his father knows, why did he hire me…us…to solve the case?"

"Maybe he didn't know then. Maybe he didn't want to believe it. Maybe he wants you to prove it to him before the police find out, so he can do something."

"What could he do?"

"Danny thinks he would send him away."

"Danny told you that?"

"Yes."

"Where to?"

"He doesn't know. But it would be too embarrassing for the church to know the minister's son burned it down. Reverend Ringer would probably lose his job."

Perhaps it was time I took this kid more seriously.

Sixteen

I was on my feet with my back to the duchess in her family's basement when I heard a click of keys and the duchess say, "Wait."

I turned, "What?"

"I got another e-mail from Danny."

"What does it say?" I asked, going back to the computer screen.

"RAED YTIREV,

MI DIARFA. WORROMOT SI HCRUHC. EH SWONK. EH SI GNIOG OT LLET. TAHW LLIW NEPPAH OT EM? I TNAW OT NUR YAWA."

I read the letters backwards and said to the duchess, "Tell him not to run away. We will come to church and protect him."

"But where will the church be? It's burned down."

"Ask Danny where they will have it."

The keyboard clicked with its almost silent sounds. We sat back and waited.

"Will the Reverend Ringer be angry if we go?" she asked.

"Angry? I think he should be glad to have people come to his church. Isn't that what it's all about?

Getting people to church?"

"But we're not going for the church part," she said.

She had a point, but I wasn't going to tell her that. "Don't you think Danny will be glad to see us?"

"I don't know."

"Let's see if he tells us where it is. If he ignores your question maybe he'd rather not have us."

"Or he ran away already."

"Did you read any of those psychology books I got you from the library?"

"All of them," she said.

I didn't know how it was possible, but I didn't argue.

It wasn't long before a voice chimed, "You've got mail," and a little mailbox appeared on her screen. A click of the mouse opened up the message.

SLWO EMOH MA01

"Owls' Home on Main Street. Ten in the morning. Let's get there early—nine-thirty, say. Can you tell him not to worry, we'll be there at nine-thirty, hang in there?" The Owls were a men's club. The Owls' Home was their club house.

I left the duchess in the basement at her computer. On the way out I waved to her mother and a new client. I walked back to the Broad Street with a small detour past the burned church, in case it gave me any ideas.

It didn't.

But after another of Clara's splendid dinners—an elegant pot roast with apple pie and ice cream for desert, and the usual teasing about serving ice cream in the dining room cutting into Clint's business in the ice cream parlor—the phone rang. Clint answered it in the kitchen and said, "It's for you, Bones."

I took the phone and barely heard the whisper on the other end. "What?" I said.

"Mr. Bones, this is Grace—Grace Ringer—Danny's mother."

"Oh, yes—sorry, I can hardly hear you."

"He's gone," she whispered hoarsely.

"Who?"

"Danny."

"Danny? He's run away?"

"He's gone with his father. But I'm scared to death something will happen."

"Is there someone with you?"

"No. They went together."

"Then why are you whispering?"

"I'm afraid Reverend Ringer might come back."

Reverend Ringer? I thought, that's her husband she's talking about. Doesn't call him Sterling? Reverend Ringer—nice and formal.

"That's what you want, isn't it?"

"What?"

"For Reverend…your husband to come back?"

There was a moment of silence. "I want Danny to come back," she said with a touch of mystery in her voice.

"Are you afraid Danny won't come back?"

"I don't know…" she said and trailed off.

"Are you saying you want Danny to come back but not the rev—your husband?"

"Oh, goodness no. I want them both back."

"Look," I said, "I'd like to talk to you about it. Can we meet somewhere?"

"Oh, no, I couldn't do that."

"Why not?"

"The reverend wouldn't like that."

"Don't tell him."

"Don't tell him? But if he comes in and sees I'm not here—what will he think?"

"That you went to the market or to see a friend. You aren't locked in, are you?"

"Nooo...but..."

"But what?" I said. "Come to the Broad Street. I'll buy you an ice cream. You can tell the reverend, if he wonders, you are here helping me with my investigation. Leave him a note so he won't worry." And, I wanted to add, you won't worry either, but I knew better. She would worry crossing the street.

"I can't," she said.

"What time do you go to church in the morning?"

"Well, when it's right here, and I just go over from the house, a few minutes before the organist starts playing. Tomorrow we're going to be at the Owls' Home.

"I'll be there at nine-thirty. We can talk..."

"Oh, dear," she said. "I fear the service..."

"Why?"

"What the reverend might say. Oh dear, I've never seen him so beside himself. He's always been able to handle anything that comes up, but Danny's just...well, he's a handful all right, and the reverend is

worried about how this is going to look in the community."

"You think he's going to say something in the
service?"

"Oh, I know he will."

"About Danny?"

"Yes."

"What will he say?"

"I don't know," she said, pronouncing her
words very slowly, "I fear he will liken Danny to
Satan."

"Will that be the end of it?"

"I don't know. I hope he doesn't hurt Danny."

"That isn't going to make him happy, is it?"

"No, but I mean physically. I wish I knew
where they were. I wish they'd come home."

"Do you want me to come over there?"

"Oh, dear, no. The reverend would be fit to be
tied if he saw you in his house when he came home."

"His house?" I asked her. "It's your house too,
isn't it?"

"No, everything is his."

"And that's all right with you?"

"He takes good care of me. I have no com-
plaints. Oh," she said, and her voice hushed even
more, "I think they're back—wait...." The phone
went silent, but I heard her footsteps scurrying about.
When she came back she said into the phone, "Yes,
he's back."

"He? Is Danny with him?"

"Yes—that's what I meant, Danny. I knew the

reverend would come back, I just wasn't sure about Danny."

"You really thought he might have hurt his son?"

"He doesn't ever call him his son. It's like they're perfect strangers sometimes."

"I've heard that," I said. "What would it take to make them friends?"

"Whoops," she whispered. I heard a door open, and she hung up the phone without saying goodbye.

Seventeen

I got to the Owls' Home the next morning at a little after nine. There was a sign announcing the church gathering at the door. I didn't want to miss anything. I was the first to arrive. It was a fine autumn morning. The leaves on the street trees were turning to rust and amber colors.

A few moments after I arrived, Casper Schultz, the church sexton, came into the empty hall—a long room—longer than it was wide.

"Find your fireboy yet, Bones?" he asked.

"Maybe," I said, looking hard into his eyes.

"Not me," he said with a gruff voice.

Casper got folding chairs out of a storage area in back and began setting them up in rows of ten with an aisle down the middle and five chairs on each side.

"I'll help you," I said, and I began bringing chairs from the back.

"No need," he said. "Got plenty of chairs."

I looked at what I thought was a small number of chairs. "How many do you need?"

"The reverend says to set up a hundred. Expects more people because of the fire—out of sympathy or something. But I don't think so. Anyway, he says put up a hundred chairs, I put up a hundred chairs."

"How many do you usually get at a Sunday service?"

"'Bout forty or fifty."

A pretty young woman came into the Owls' with a camera around her neck.

"Is Reverend Ringer here?" she asked.

"Not yet," Casper Schultz said, frowning at her camera. "But I can tell you he isn't going to take kindly to big newspaper stories."

"Oh, I'm just from the local paper. Nothing big. But there is some interest in the community."

"Won't want the service disrupted with pictures."

"That's all right. I can just take a few before it starts. I'm not going to write anything unfavorable…"

"Well, suit yourself. You can talk to Reverend Ringer when he gets here."

"And his son?" she said. "Will he be here?"

"I expects. Usually sits with his mother in the front row."

Oh my, I thought, the word is out already. That's what happens in a small town. Well, at least the big city paper hasn't come.

People started trickling in. The Reverend and Mrs. Sterling Ringer and Danny came in around nine-thirty.

Casper Schultz rolled out a small piano and set it in front of the first row and off to the side. "This look right to you, Reverend?" he asked Sterling

Ringer, who looked over the set up and said, "Fine."

Reverend Ringer moseyed on to the back room, where he could be out of sight to make his dramatic appearance at the start of the service.

I moved quickly over to the reverend's wife Grace and her son Danny.

"How did it go last night?" I asked, glancing at Danny.

Grace pursed her lips. "We're alive," she said.

Danny's face was glum and impassive. He was no longer hopping from foot to foot in that impetuous dance of his. I saw no bubble gum in his mouth. You could have told he had been adopted by the absence of the big-as-all-outdoors smile his father had. Danny this morning was one glum puppy. But all my efforts to find out what went on the night before failed.

Looking across the room, I noticed our newspaper woman had put her camera out of sight, probably in her purse, and had decided against pushing for pictures before the service. Maybe because she thought she'd be put out of the service and miss her story if she did so.

The congregation and some apparent visitors gathered and filled barely half of the hundred chairs Casper Schultz had set up.

Just as the organist sat at the piano—a serious comedown from her electronic organ, which perished in the fire along with everything else—the door opened, and the duchess stepped inside and stopped, her eyes traveling over the scene as though she had just stepped from the bright sun into the darkness of a movie theater.

I waved to her, but she didn't respond. She searched until her eyes settled on Danny. She went up to him and squeezed his arm without saying anything I could hear. Then she released him, and he and his mother took their seats as the only ones in the front row.

The duchess and I sat behind them. The organist did her best with the piano, which was badly out of tune—the Owls probably not knowing the difference at their parties, which could get loud enough to drown out anyone who tried to play the piano.

When she finished her Prelude, the Reverend Sterling Ringer made his entrance from the door in front of us. He was carrying his Bible in one hand and his hymnal in the other.

"Let us pray," he said, with his big smile unflinching.

I expected some reference to the fire in his prayer, but there was none. It was a prayer he could have given at a pancake breakfast sponsored by the Boy Scouts.

He then moved behind a lectern, which the sexton must have put there without me seeing it. It was directly in front of his wife and Danny.

"Well, friends," he said, "It's been quite a week for our struggling church. So be it. Jesus struggled mightily, and he endured. We will endure. I'll say that! I'm sorry we don't have any hymnals for you, as they burned along with everything else in the tragic—man-made—fire." He looked down at Danny, who was struggling not to squirm in his seat.

"I guess we are lucky we didn't perish in the

fire, and that the Ringer family is intact. My wife Grace is here with our adopted child Danny—and we can be grateful for that."

I thought I heard a low groan from the duchess, who was sitting still as a statue beside me.

"We will rebuild, of course," Reverend Ringer was saying from behind his lectern. "It will take some doing. Our insurance, we discovered, was woefully inadequate to cover the cost of replacement. We will hope our friends in the community will offer some aid, but they have many demands on their time and money. This is the message I have been getting from those who were good enough to offer their sympathy for our difficulty.

"Now, since we have no hymnals, I have tried to pick hymns we are all familiar with—but if you don't know the words, just hum along or sing 'ah'. It's important that we raise our voices to the Lord to help see us through these sad and difficult times."

The first hymn was *The Church's One Foundation*.

"One foundation?" the duchess whispered to me after the piano introduction had started, "That's all that's left—the foundation."

After we got the music out of the way—and not that many people knew the words, there were a lot of ahs and hmms—Reverend Ringer said, "Friends, it's time for your testimonies to the Lord. Say anything that's on your mind. I want to help you as well as all of us."

He looked at Danny, who didn't move. Grace Ringer took a huge intake of breath, but she didn't move or look at Danny. She stared straight ahead at her husband's knees as near as I could tell.

Then I was startled to feel a stir beside me. I looked at the duchess, and she was slowly getting to her feet. She just stood there for a long time without saying anything, as though she were collecting her thoughts. Then, without facing the audience, those thoughts came tumbling out over Danny's head.

"How hard is it to show love between a father and a son? The father wants to be a stern figure—a teacher, an example in the son's life. Perhaps the father's own childhood was sad and disappointing, full of rebellion or suppressed rebellion.

"The fear that one is adopted is common among children. Parents can lessen these fears, or they can promulgate them depending on their own predilections."

The duchess was showing, among other things, her particular type of highly developed intelligence. She was repeating word-for-word in her monotone voice, which sounded like she was reading words she didn't understand. Indeed, I wasn't sure this twelve year old knew that promulgate meant make known or prompt, even encourage and that predilection meant a liking. She was quoting word-for-word the library psychology books I got for her.

"A twelve year old boy may be afraid of his father, who is idealistic, strict and demanding of the boy but has never shown him any affection. He never got any affection when he was a boy and doesn't know how to show it.

"A boy's attitude toward his father could be

repressed so the boy couldn't show anger toward his father even though he was often severely punished.

"The son longs for the affection and approval of his father at the same time he feels hostile toward him.

"This has made some boys very religious. If the boy's parents are very religious, it can make the boy rebel and reject the religion of his father.

"One can imagine a son of a minister feels so powerless he might even attempt to burn the church where his father preaches. Maybe it started as an accident—or it was just meant to scare his father, to get some attention for the boy by making some walls black. But it spread so fast the boy couldn't put it out and had to run to save his life.

"Maybe no one saw the boy because there was a door inside the church to the inside of the house, and his parents were watching television with their backs to the door. So the boy was in his room when the fire was first noticed.

"Sometimes nature limits us—makes us so we cannot do all the things we want to do, so we can't get others to like us like we'd like them to. Fathers are busy people, and sometimes they don't have time for their sons, and their sons don't understand this. Sometimes sons do extreme things to gain attention. Maybe they get out of hand. Maybe the boy is sorry. But the communication between father and son is so little that the truth can never come out. The father is too angry and the boy is too scared.

"Danny didn't want to burn the church down. He was grounded for talking back to his father—his father who never calls him his son, who always says he is adopted, implying that he isn't really his son.

"But Danny wants to be your son. Everybody needs an identity. He reached out for attention—not in a good way this time, but the only way he saw. He found gasoline and rags in the basement of the church. He thought about scaring his folks with a small fire. It got away from him. He's very sorry. He didn't want to burn the church down, he only wanted a father."

The duchess stayed standing looking straight ahead at nobody. The reverend, who had stood for her testimony, was seeing the duchess and the congregation through his tears. The silence was abruptly broken by applause, which I joined. The photographer slipped over to the side, where she took the duchess's picture.

I tugged at the duchess's sleeve to get her to sit down. She finally did, and the applause got louder.

Eighteen

Reverend Sterling Ringer looked dumbfounded standing in front of the small, vigorously applauding congregation. He tried out his famous smile once or twice, but it seemed to have failed him. I suppose he was considering his options, and there weren't that many good ones.

He could signal to stop the applause, but that would be ungracious. It would seem small, like he wasn't willing to share the attention.

He could go to his speaker's stand and change the subject, make believe the duchess had not given her speech, but that would seem odd, especially since the event had gotten such an enthusiastic response.

He could acknowledge the 'testimony' from 'sister' Verity, give it faint praise, then move on with his sermon.

Instead, when the applause finally stopped, Reverend Ringer, standing behind the lectern the Owls' Home had provided him, said, "I won't be giving a sermon this morning." He paused a moment, thoughtfully, then added, "I feel it has already been given."

There was some laughter, then more applause. "Verity," he said. "Would you please stand up and turn around to see what a wonderful impression you made."

The duchess seemed shocked, but she dutifully stood, turned around and let loose with her biggest smile, which was very small indeed.

The applause welled up again. It was so loud I thought I was at a rock concert.

I think the duchess would have stood there all day and the applause would have continued had I not tugged at her sleeve and told her to sit.

"Well," the reverend said, "That was quite a reception. A well-deserved one, I'll say that."

The reverend looked over at the first row. "Danny," he said, "Come up here... if you will." He held out his hand to the boy. From where I sat, I wouldn't say Danny was too happy about going to the front and facing all those people. He looked like he thought he was going to get one of his father's great scoldings—probably be grounded in public for years.

Finally, after an embarrassing wait, forcing the reverend to beckon again with his hands, Danny stood up and took the few difficult steps, like a wooden soldier, to the lectern, where his father waited, his big-as-all-outdoors smile broadening, if you can believe it.

Danny was moving as slowly as a zombie, and when he arrived at his father he didn't turn to face the audience. He just stood still, his face toward his father but without looking up into that big face that was smiling down on him.

"Here," the reverend said, "Stand by my side and look out at the folks. I want them to get a good look at you."

When Danny slowly turned he was one glum, unhappy camper, waiting for the boom to fall on him.

"Friends," the reverend said, "and Danny, religion means many things to many people. There's one thing, though, you can't have a religion without—two things really—one is forgiveness, and I want to publicly forgive Danny for the unfortunate…circumstances these past days, and I want to say to Danny, 'I forgive you—and I hope in exchange, you will forgive me.'"

In front of us, Grace gasped, then reached for her handkerchief.

Danny did not know what to make of his father, but from the look on his face he was expecting a trick.

"I guess it's no secret, and no small thanks to Verity—our beloved Verity Buscador, I'll say that—but it's no secret I have been stingy about calling Danny what he is—what he most certainly is, I realized this morning, and that is…my son.

"Ladies and gentlemen, sisters and brothers in our Lord, I want to introduce you to my son, Danny."

Now, in front of us, Grace collapsed into a full blubber, and her handkerchief was not big enough to soak up all the tears.

The audience burst into applause and rose to their feet, pleasing the reverend to no end and surprising and confusing Danny, who looked as though he had just heard something that had to be good, but he wasn't sure why. I think Danny was still thinking this was a buildup for a bigger let down later. Perhaps, when they got home, his father would give him a lifetime grounding.

"Thank you, sisters and brothers in the Lord," the Reverend Sterling Ringer beamed. "This is a new beginning for us, a fresh start, I'll say that. We're going to rebuild our church. It isn't going to be easy or cheap, but we'll be out there working with our hands and our hearts, me right along side my son Danny here, and I hope and pray you will join us in this great effort."

There was a cheer and more applause. Then, as though he had just gotten a bright idea, the reverend said, "Tell you what, let's all meet at the Broad Street Ice Cream Parlor after the service. We'll talk about the rebuilding of our beloved church—and you—all of you are beloved too, I'll say that.

"Now, let's sing *Onward Christian Soldiers*, then we can march proudly up to the Broad Street."

Danny started to return to his seat. The reverend put a hand out to stop him. "Stay up here with me, son."

Nineteen

I was frankly surprised at the number of the congregation that came along to the Broad Street Hotel and Clint's Ice Cream Parlor. I got goose pimples to see us all in a group, marching with a purpose.

Danny walked with the duchess, and he didn't seem put out at her talk. I think he realized it was what turned his father around.

I still had some friends and contacts in Juvenile Probation. I knew Danny's punishment was not going to be easy, but I was going to do what I could for him to see that it was fair.

Our newspaper reporter interviewed Danny and the duchess on our way. I think it made them feel important.

When we arrived inside the ice cream parlor Clint's jaw dropped open. It was clear there were more people than Clint had seats. Attracted by the noise of all those people, Clara came in and soon talked a group into the dining room.

I was sitting at a small table beside the reverend, Danny, Grace and the duchess. People were coming to praise the duchess left and right, and I hoped she wouldn't get a big head about it.

People were also coming to offer to help in the

rebuilding of the church—even those who didn't belong to the church and who might have come to the service at Owls' Home out of curiosity.

The crowd was too large for Clint and Clara to handle, so I pitched in taking orders and scooping ice cream and being an all-around good waiter.

When I went to the reverend's table to take their order, he smiled, and his bow tie was bobbing again when he said, "Bones, I'm pleased with the way your assignment turned out. I will pay as promised."

I got a lump in my throat. I had half expected him to say he didn't have the money or would have to take a special collection. Then I wondered if I should offer to donate my fee to the rebuilding of the church, but I was so short of cash since I left the police department, I thought I'd better take the money. It wasn't going to be that much anyway. I was going to give the duchess a share besides.

But then when I started to get tips I didn't expect, I announced I was donating all my tips to the church rebuilding, thinking—when I thought about it at all—that my tips wouldn't pay a carpenter for an hour.

A funny thing happened, suddenly instead of getting fifty cents and a dollar or so, I was getting twenty dollars—fifty dollars—even a hundred dollars from the pharmacist, who was a Lutheran.

I took them directly to Reverend Ringer, who was so pleased his big smile made his bow tie dance.

When Clint came to the reverend's table Reverend Ringer tried to pay him, but Clint held up a hand, "Your money's no good here today," he said.

"That goes for the whole table." He looked at his granddaughter with a warm smile. "I hear you were the star of the service, Verity. I'm so proud of you."

The duchess could have smiled, I couldn't be sure.

"Clint, I thank you for your generosity. We all thank you—Grace, Verity, and my son Danny. Clint, you know my son Danny, don't you?"

Clint smiled, "I may have known him before you did."

That stopped the reverend, he frowned trying to understand, then nodded, smiled and with his bow tie bobbing, said, "Those days are behind us."

"Reverend," Clint said, " I have a contractor owes me some money—and some favors. I'm going to send him over there. He'll take the project in hand. Get yourself some volunteers here."

The reverend said, "Good idea, very good—I'll say that!" The Reverend Ringer stood and made an eloquent call for help. "We're going to do whatever we can, whatever's needed, to rebuild our church to continue to serve this wonderful community."

I think almost everyone in the place came over to the table, and Grace took out a piece of paper from her purse and made it a sign-up sheet.

We started that afternoon, cleaning up the mess.

The local trash man sent a big bin for us to throw the rubble in, even though it was Sunday.

Even Minnie Werner from across the street came over to see what all the fuss was about, and she pitched in as best she could, though she did have some trouble bending over.

The contractor pulled up in his pick-up truck and told Reverend Ringer Clint had called him, and he was here to work on the plans. "Won't cost you a cent," he said. "I owe Clint big time."

The reverend beamed, "And I owe his grand-daughter, Verity here, big time."

Verity was pleased, I could tell. The smile couldn't match the reverend's but she was throwing rubble in that bin at a rapid pace.

Danny was by her side picking up burned wood and fallen bricks and taking them to the dumpster. He paused near the reverend, and the contractor and the Reverend Ringer stopped.

"Oh, Bill, I want you to meet Danny," he beamed, "my son."

An Excerpt from
To Oz and Back: A Bones and the Duchess Mystery
by Alexandra Eden

By the time the duchess came down the sidewalk with this strange looking kid, I had resolved very little. The news from the FBI and local police was not encouraging, and I couldn't really say I had done better. I had only left my rocking chair for lunch, and I didn't want to leave it when the duchess and her friend came up the steps and walked right by me into the hotel without saying hello or anything. I wondered if she saw me at all. I think she did, and was just not aware I was anyone she knew. That was one of the things about the duchess—she didn't react to you the way other people did.

I followed them into the dining room where they were setting up shop on the middle table. I suggested we move to the corner to be out of everyone's way, but they ignored me.

"Is this your friend?" I asked the duchess, hinting for an introduction.

"Yes," she said.

"Hi," I said to the boy, who was taking a laptop computer out of his backpack. "I'm Bones Fatzinger."

"Hi," he said, without supplying *his* name.

"What's your name?" I asked.

"Calvin."

"Oh—Calvin what?"

He didn't answer right away—then he said, "Just Calvin." He had a strange crooked smile on his thin, pink lips. He wore a tee-shirt that had been tie-dyed shades of purple and blue, rumpled short pants, and a necktie over the tee-shirt. The tie was not tied like a real necktie—more like a shoelace that didn't quite make it. His eyes were hidden behind a large pair of eyeglasses with rims like a leopard's spots.

He set up his laptop on the table—opened it and turned it on, then began speaking as though he were instructing a convention of code breakers.

"We began in the standard way, of studying the groups of letters and numbers for patterns we might recognize as common words for names—Wanda has five letters, and the second and the fifth letters are the same. Arvilla has seven letters—the first and last are not only the same, they are the same as the second and fifth letter of Wanda. So, we looked for five and seven letter words with those patterns—especially in the beginning and end of the notes. We might expect one to begin, 'Dear Wanda,' another, 'Dear Arvilla.' They might end with the names after some ending, like 'Yours in secret' or something."

"There is also the double 'l' in Arvilla," the duchess chimed in.

"Oh, yes," Calvin said. "Sometimes there is a symbol or number substituted for double letters. Two l's in Arvilla might be L2, DL for double L. Two O's in book could be eyes crossed. You can make a code any-way you want, as long as everyone who uses the code knows what it means."

"Do we know that Wanda got any of these codes? Did we ever look for anything there?" I asked, knowing the answer.

"I called Mrs. Trexler," the duchess said, sur-prising me with her initiative, "she said there were papers in her room like these—" she pointed at the code scratchings, "but she cleaned up and threw them away."

I groaned.

"But maybe these are *from* her, and what was thrown away were notes from Wanda."

"It's beginning to look like they ran away together, and the codes were the way they planned it and told each other about it," I said.

"Maybe," the duchess said.

"Maybe not," Nerd Calvin said. "The simplest code is to reverse the letters—A is Z and Z is A. B is Y and Y is B—" I wondered if he was going through the whole alphabet to make his point. "I programmed that and nothing came up."

"Another way is to slip a letter or a number in them. You can put the key at the beginning of the sentence in numbers. For example, start a sentence with four, and A becomes D, B is E and so forth—or you can put the four upside down, or with a zero in front or a line through it—anything to show it's different and A becomes W, B becomes V and the like."

"That's very impressive, Calvin," I said, giving the kid his due. "So what concrete conclusions have you come to? Like about what the notes mean?"

He looked glum. "Nothing yet," he said, "but Verity and I are working on it."

"How about if we turn the notes over to the FBI?"

"No!" the duchess said. "I found them—the FBI didn't do anything. I'm going to solve it."

"*You?*" I said. "This is my case."

"Well, okay," she said. "Then you solve it first. You have the same notes."

"Okay," I said. "I'll make a deal. Take one more

116

day. If we don't have anything by then, we show the FBI. They have professionals that do this for a living. They could probably solve it in five minutes."

I couldn't get them to agree to that. It didn't matter. If they didn't solve it in one more day, *I* would take the notes to the FBI.

In the meantime, I might go back to talk to Grumbera at the local police station around the corner. Hint around. See how he felt about codes. All these scratchings from Arvilla's bedroom could be a blind alley—an alley you can go into, but there is no way out of.

"One more day," I repeated, but neither the duchess nor the nerd responded. They were too busy trying to solve the puzzle of the code.

ALLEN A. KNOLL, PUBLISHERS
Established 1989

We are a small press located in Santa Barbara, Ca,
specializing in
books for intelligent people who read for fun.

Please visit our website at www.knollpublishers.com
for a complete catalog, scintilating sample chapters,
in depth interviews, and thought-provoking
reading guides.

Or call (800) 777-7623 to receive a catalog
and/or be kept informed of new releases.